More Praise for John O'Brien

for *Better*

"No contemporary novelist has plumbed so deeply into the human heart, and none has paid a steeper price for visiting those depths than John O'Brien. *Better* shows us what America lost when the author of *Leaving Las Vegas* took his own life. Unflinching, dark-souled, cry-until-you-laugh authentic . . . each word of this novel burns as true and doomed as a lit match dropped in a shot of whiskey. John O'Brien was a writer who lived and died with every sentence. *Better* is testament to the miracle of what the man accomplished—and what he might have accomplished had not death seemed like a better alternative. No one who reads this book will walk away unmoved."
—Jerry Stahl, author of *Permanent Midnight* and *Pain Killers*

for *Leaving Las Vegas*

"O'Brien has a strong tradition behind him . . . that of American natural-ism, and he fits into it well. From Stephen Crane to Hubert Selby, Jr. . . . [O'Brien] achieves real power in his writing. You seldom encounter it anymore, but when you do you know you've been properly whacked by a real talent."
—*New York Daily News*

"John O'Brien was a stunningly talented writer who created poetry from the most squalid materials." —Jay McInerney, author of *Brightness Falls*

"John O'Brien has a very great talent."
—Larry Brown, author of *Joe* and *Big Bad Love*

for *The Assault on Tony's*

"O'Brien's singular voice . . . survives, taking us deep into an alcoholic's world that few others have described so well." —*New York Times Book Review*

"O'Brien's essential voice [is] brave, riffingly brilliant, celebratory, and doomed."
—*Time Out New York*

"Metaphorically rich and remarkably smart." —*Cleveland Magazine*

Better

Better

a novel by
John O'Brien

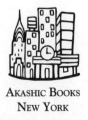

AKASHIC BOOKS
NEW YORK

Published by Akashic Books
© 2009 by the Estate of John O'Brien

ISBN-13: 978-1-933354-82-8
Library of Congress Control Number: 2008937349

First printing

Akashic Books
PO Box 1456
New York, NY 10009
info@akashicbooks.com
www.akashicbooks.com

PROLOGUE

Start that long climb again, oh hapless paperboy, working your reiterative way up the hill and down the hill, over and over, day in and day out, load of newspapers nothing more than a wire basket full of trouble to be toted along the line to some mythical vacation in Hawaii, perhaps a weekend in Disney World. How very unfortunate for you to be sentenced by the whim and wealth of your parents to a hellish route of sparsely placed, hillside-nestled palaces of paper readers. The cards are stacked against you, for your faceless nemesis, some chubby little Mexican kid in the flat and dusty grid of Fontana, will undoubtedly be sucking on Mickeysicles and Florida sun, a "Carrier of the Month" certificate in for framing at the Art-N-Such back home, while you're still working out leg cramps.

Of course I could be completely naïve; my familiarity with paperboys and what they pine for is admittedly dated. For all I know this kid is casing houses, scoping out car stereos, or simply earning an honest dollar for a weekend trip to the outdoor drugstores which lie somewhat nearer the heart of Los Angeles. Rougher places of night, where the capitalists are even younger than himself, the work even more demanding.

I only know of such places from high-contrast videotape on local news programs, but I imagine the neighborhood around here is a little easier to get through, a little more unctuous. Of course I can't be sure, for the house I'm in doesn't fit that mold. At least I don't think it does, and the neighborhood around here is, in truth, not well known to me either. So many things are not well known to me, where I live is simply another one of those. Yesterday I happened to glance out the window (not a habit) and I saw a guy leading his family on a walk, an after-dinner stroll. Four of them. Lost in conversation, they'd wandered up our little driveway, hands in jeans, some front, some rear, one in the pocket of another's jeans. They'd wandered up our little driveway, and though I'd never seen any of them before, I knew they lived nearby.

I was in no mood for trouble, but if I had been I would have swung wide the window and called out an ambivalent "Hiyahey!" just to watch their faces simultaneously lock into the presumptuous grin of glad-to-finally-meet-you-we-live-nearby-so-it's-okay-in-fact-our-menials-may-know-your-menials. Some hands would have quickly been yanked out of pocket, most notably the one that was in the other's. The guy in charge would have rapidly assessed the situation, silently debating whether or not I could be trusted to understand his implicit right as a fellow well-off homeowner to wander amiably onto the property of his fellow, well off the beaten path. Wifey might have considered whatever she had heard from other neighbors and pondered the wisdom of such a contact. The young pocket twins, while awaiting instruction, would have thought about when they could tactfully reestablish pocket contact. I would have said nothing, remained silent for a beat and watched them squirm, waited patiently for that first inevitable whisper amongst themselves. Then I would have cut them off sharply, stifled my own cue and said,

CHAPTER ONE

Double Felix is semireclined. From where I stand—perhaps ten feet behind him—I can hear the whine of his headphones, excess noise that even his ears cannot collect. True to form, he has the volume control of his tape player set too high, but I won't mention this to him; Double Felix is the sort of person who resents concern, or so he claims. Anyway, disturbing him is rarely a good idea, so I turn and walk from the room.

"I see you, William," I hear him yell after me. "I see your fat fucking face reflected in the window."

Rather than respond to that, I pull shut his door and continue down the hall. I should mention here that "your fat fucking face" is merely one of Double Felix's many terms of endearment. My face, as well as the rest of me, is angular, almost gaunt. I have the sort of face that one expects to be adorned with a modicum of gratuitous facial hair, perhaps an anemic goatee, or an adolescent mustache, though I do not and would never have either. I did once spend some time with a black glass marker and a mirror; the effect was unconvincing.

Passing the familiar array of six doors, two of which stand open, I arrive at the end of the hall where I exit to the deck. Here I will stay until morning—a relatively new habit of mine—feeling the airborne chill of the Pacific Ocean sweep over my body, linger in seductive spirals, and grow ever more to the point as it waits for sleep to take me. It is then, as I lie innocently, making stupid barks and gurgles in protest to my dreams, it is then that the wind will turn malicious and send its bite to my bones. I will awaken and shiver, clutch myself and curse. Though the door behind me is unlocked and a bed awaits in my name, I will stay here and watch for the sky to lighten.

In the morning I will join Double Felix for vodka on his balcony. We will have our regular palaver, perhaps joined briefly by one of the female houseguests wearing one of Double Felix's shirts, or an outcall hooker clad in lace and wondering if Double Felix meant it when he asked her to move in. "Do you live here too?" she will ask of me, her eyes searching mine for either a clue or a warning sign. "What has Double Felix been telling you?" I will respond, trying to look mischievous. Seeing I want to sleep with her, Double Felix will then chuckle, and so give his blessing.

Our house—I mean his house, for we are all guests of Double Felix, myself the most tenacious—sits on a cliff in Los Angeles, overlooking the Pacific, just northwest of the city of Santa Monica. Most of the nearby roads are known as canyons, circuitous strips of black and yellow cut to deferentially follow nature's compelling leads, and I have yet to find a straight line that leads here, much less a shortest distance. It is my understanding that Double Felix purchased this house some years ago. I would have sworn he built it himself, for it matches him and he it to a degree seemingly beyond coincidence; but perhaps that can be only a result of a chance purchase, as no man could possibly know himself that well. I can't say exactly why I find this house so appropriate for Double Felix, but I do know I feel very much an element in whatever it is he has wrought here.

Taken as a piece of real estate it may not be overwhelming, but it is certainly atypical. None of the rooms resemble actual shapes—the type that are found in geometry texts and mimicked in most construction; no, these rooms are squashed-pointed ovals and semicircular rhomboids. The largest room, referred to as "the big room" by Double Felix, is the part of the house that one enters. It spans almost the entire length of the house on the inland side, and so has no ocean view. Between it and the cliff, starting on the right or north, are: Double Felix's bedroom and private balcony; six guest rooms, each with walled, private balconies; and a large wooden deck. All these are connected through ornate double doors to a long hallway which ends on the south side of the house at the kitchen, an industrial-looking place full of cast-iron and aluminum cookware hanging from immense steel racks; all of it, like the kitchen itself, about twice as large and half as busy as it needs to be. Outside, there is no yard or landscaping, and barely enough blacktop to qualify as a driveway under local ordinances. We are as remote as one can be in this area, due mostly to the huge fence that runs the perimeter. We live in relative seclusion from the nearby residents.

Of course, accommodations such as these are not cheap to acquire or to maintain, especially for a man with no apparent means of support. My concern about this matter, and indeed my interest, has long since vanished, but back before the basis of our arrangement became clear to me, I was insanely curious about the source of Double Felix's wealth, which, judging by his immoderate generosity, I imagined to be substantial. "Double Felix," I said, marching into his bedroom very early one morning, "if I'm going to agree to live here at your expense [he had recently made the offer—actually it was always there, on the table, as it were, and he just confirmed it verbally] then I must insist on knowing something about the source of my good fortune. I must know how you pay for all of this." I folded my arms and glared at him, trying to look as though this matter of honor and integrity, if not resolved, would send me marching off without a damn into a filmic fog. "William," he responded, tired and amused as always, lifting his head from between the legs of a girl whom I did not recognize, "what follows is a list of facts. Please listen without responding or reacting, and when I am done reciting this list, please leave my bedroom and allow me to finish what I have started here. One: you needn't agree to live here. Two: if you wish to stay you will make me happy. Three: this house is for your use. Four: you may inquire about my assets as often as you wish without fear of angering me, but I will never acknowledge your questions. Five: we have money, and I am always happy to give you some. Six: you are feeling concern over issues within yourself that will one day seem trivial to you. Seven: you are not here because of my money, but only one of us knows that." He stopped. Turning back to the waiting vagina, he paused. "Thank you for your time, William. Please leave now and return for Morning Vodka in sixty minutes." And I did just that.

Double Felix's bedroom, where he spends much of his time during the day either preparing for or recovering from one of his many naps, and where even now he sits with his legs crossed at the knees and his ears in the delicate forcepslike pinch of his featherweight Japanese headphones, is more or less in the shape of a teardrop; no, a half-teardrop; better yet, like the cross section of a runaway drop of lab mercury that has just been fecklessly prodded by a spoon in the hands of a red-faced student; asymmetrical, flat and round, found and made. The wall that is curved most overtly is really just a series of oversized windows that stretch from the floor to the ceiling and look out on the ocean. There are also two glass doors which open to Double Felix's private balcony, and it is here where he and I spend our mornings. The decor is simple and the room sparsely furnished, though in the context of these things it is clear that no expense has been spared. There is only his bed, two overstuffed lounge chairs, a small table, a built-in bar, and an immense but uncluttered steel desk that holds a single lamp and several neatly kept stacks of papers. Double Felix forbids anyone—including me—to look at these papers, and I at least have always respected his wishes.

Double Felix loves his bedroom, and spends much of his life there, though he is not totally reclusive. I think he feels it is the one place in his house that he has reserved for himself, that he has total control over. I say this because the only times that I can recall him being moved to anger were when the evening's festivities spilled out of the big room and into his bedroom. Many times I have seen Double Felix crowded in some remote corner of the kitchen, trying to have a conversation through the pushing, shoving, crowding chaos of one of our parties. But he tolerates this rather than retreat to his vast, empty bedroom and risk leading the crowd along with him. Thus he swallows whole the confusion along with the rest of us. Once or twice, when unusually drunk, he has even forbidden himself from entering, choosing instead to nap in an empty guest room. (He has never told me this; I draw the conclusion strictly from my own surreptitious observations.)

The big room is a place to find someone, and Double Felix often drifts in for light talk and television. Though actual parties do not occur all that often, Double Felix keeps enough guests in the house to maintain a nice selection of talking/eating/sleeping partners, and the big room is the hub. Double Felix has referred to it as "the place from which we commence our satellite activities." A full wet bar runs the length of the shortest of the two straight walls; the third and longest wall runs in concavity from the room, carrying with it Double Felix's collection of erotic murals, painted tastefully and adeptly by a talented former guest whom I never met. The room is replete with high-end consumer electronics, offering more ways to view a video image or listen to one's favorite audio medium than could be exhausted in a week. Double Felix enjoys this equipment and insists on installing it himself—he is surprisingly skillful with tools—yet he is the first to laugh it off should a clumsy or drunken guest damage something accidentally. "Time for an upgrade!" he might say, placing his arm around the embarrassed culprit and leading him to a topic changer. More than anything, Double Felix hates to see people feeling uncomfortable or bad about something, especially something as trivial as a stereo or a television.

Across the hall from the big room are the six guest rooms; in fact, mine is the door that lies directly opposite the door to the big room. Nearest the deck (Double Felix moved me there in an attempt to lure me back to sleeping inside), it is virtually identical to the other five guest rooms. Long, narrow, chutelike areas, they each have a private bath on the hall side and a walled balcony on the ocean side; simple furnishings, a queen-size bed, a full bar, and the usual electronic conveniences, including a private telephone line. I have known guests to spend days in these rooms, their through-the-door acknowledgments to Double Felix's daily "how ya doin'" knock serving as their only interaction with the rest of us.

"What is this garbage?" I asked Double Felix one day, exasperated that he should be so willing to support a particular guest who had rarely blessed us with his presence. "It's all right, William," he said. "These things don't last forever. Besides, where else could he get away with this?" "Well, we're not running a detox ward here," I responded. "Exactly," he said. As with so many of my complaints to Double Felix, this left me feeling ashamed, and I retreated to my room, where later that night I first got the idea of sleeping on the deck.

On the deck I watch blink from my view the last, tiny, optically illusory, rapidly plunging, floating little oval of the sun's tippy-top, leaving the residual glow of dusk. I hear activity from inside the house, from the big room; but there is no party tonight—no major party—just the regular gathering of the guests and any friends that they may have clinging around. Like socks out of the dryer, these friends can be, often staying way too late and doing their best to remain inconspicuous, only to be eventually discovered and pulled from under a sweater or off the ass side of someone's panties. I stand and walk to the bar out here, mix myself a gin, and regard my usual chaise lounge. It is getting uncomfortable as the supporting straps, unaccustomed to the overtime, stretch past the intended parameters of the frame. I shall have to find the courage to rotate to another; there are many to choose from out here. Sunny days find this space filled with hungover men and bare-breasted women. Content with the moment, though undoubtedly preoccupied with more eventful or promising ones, they recline and take their solar nourishment, consider the sublime curse of this place that has found them. Indeed, a deck full of the sort of women Double Felix keeps about the place can be a most distracting sight. Many are only too happy to embrace this environment with its condoned nudity and promiscuity, and though I have never witnessed what would normally be called an orgy on the premises, there have been times when I've been awakened by and invited to join an overly responsive coital couple enjoying the cool air of my outdoor sleeping quarters; but that is not my style. I have known women of my own selection on this deck, though I prefer to limit those activities to my room and reserve this, inasmuch as I can, as my own private plenum. Simple oak, some superfluous reclining apparatus, an abundance of gin, a rail of no substance, this is where I sleep; it is outside the house.

"William?"

A voice from behind, accompanied by the familiar click of the French doors, beckons. It is Laurie, our most recent housemate. She came to us as a friend of a friend at the last big party and simply failed to leave afterward. Double Felix, discovering her on a sofa the next day, offered her the use of one of the two empty rooms. This was to the surprise of no one as Laurie is quite fetching, though that is not strictly a prerequisite for an invitation by him. That was two days ago, and I suspect that Laurie, enjoying herself, is feeling guilty about not yet sleeping with Double Felix—I happen to know she hasn't—but again, this is not required behavior.

"Laurie dear," I say, not yet turning, hoping that my quick recognition of her voice will be impressive, "what can I do for you tonight?"

Diffidently she steps toward me, almost tiptoeing. "I'm sorry to bother you out here—I understand that this is your space—but you seem to be close to Double Felix, and I was hoping I could ask you something."

I turn to face her and am struck by her genuine beauty. Her long brown hair, looking an exquisite mess, looking like it's always disheveled as if by design, dances in the breeze. Like so many interesting women she looks at once the daughter and the mother, an expression of simple acceptance and complex pride governing her even features, sparring with a very real sexuality that she seems not quite comfortable with.

"No, no," I say, "I have a room. I merely sleep out here, but you are always welcome." Motioning her to follow, I spin back to my chaise and sit on its end, a regrettably condescending pat falling from my palm onto the vacant spot beside me. "Drink?" I ask stupidly, as if this offer is the reason I walked away from the bar to the chaise.

"Just a sip of yours."

This is a good sign. She seats herself next to me, and now very encouraged, I say, "You know, Laurie, I'm very glad you've decided to spend some time with us. I think you'll find Double Felix to be an accommodating host."

I think I see a frown skate across her face. I must sound stupid, that solicitous talking-to-a-girl quality in my voice. Even I can hear it. I haven't heard myself like this for years, and I wonder what it is about Laurie that raises this unfortunate, boyish ghost in me.

"And you?" she says. "How will I find you to be, William?" This is no doubt just a bit of sugar for my coffee, nothing to get excited about.

"Approachable," I say, predictably excited nevertheless, furthering my reckless pursuit of a starring role in some future derisive gossip between Laurie and her friends: *Approachable*! *He actually said "approachable"!* So evoked, I'll be a moment's entertainment amidst the doughnuts and titters of some ritualistic slumber party.

She gives me that polite look that I'm convinced is taught in pretty-girl school, the one that says: Oh PLEASE! Is there no end to what I must tolerate? "I'll keep that in mind," she says. "Actually, the reason I'm out here pestering you is . . ."

"Yes," I jump quickly in, relieved to be moving along to safer ground even if it is behind-the-back, possible defaming talk of my only friend; we men know no loyalty to each other in the face of a pretty girl. "You mentioned that you had a question about Double Felix. I have of a lot of them myself, but you're right, I do know him as well as anybody." I sip from my glass then hold it out to her.

She regards it and says, "Why does everybody call him Double Felix? I mean let's face it, that's a strange name. Why not just Felix?" Her hand goes out for my glass then pulls back ever so slightly without touching it, her knee twitching impatiently.

I get the impression that she really doesn't care about my answer, but I want to come up with a good one anyway. Unfortunately I don't have one, and fumbling again, I say, "I have never known him to respond to any other address." I return my glass to my own lips, a little dismayed at the emptiness of this truth.

"How long have you known him?" she asks, decidedly not dismayed.

Sticky. "Two . . . three years. I guess I moved in about three years ago." I relate this with a thoughtful wrinkle in my eye, as if the years have gone heretofore unsummed, and I'm only now realizing that so much of my otherwise busy life has slipped away.

She seems surprised at my response and now indicates that she would like a sip of my gin. "Are you sleeping with him?" she wants to know.

This question always annoys me, though somehow, coming from her, it's not so bad. I decide to be cryptic nonetheless. "Well, we generally stay off of each other's hit list, if that's what you mean."

She blinks, dropping it. Next: "Three years, huh? Do you pay him rent or anything? Of course, this is none of my business."

"No, but whether or not we're sleeping together is your business, right?" This sounds a little harder than I'd intended, but it's discouraging to have a girl you're flirting with suddenly ask you if you're sleeping with another man. I must be getting bitchy, so I smile broadly and say, "Double Felix just likes my company. It's true that I have turned out to be the most permanent of his guests—as far as I know—but no, I don't pay any more rent than you do. He and I have long since come to terms with all of that." I surrender my drink to her.

Without drinking, happy to be in temporary control of the glass, she says, "It all seems very cozy, but you must feel a little strange, right? I mean, there must be tension sometimes. Does he ever pull rank? Does he ever ask anyone to leave? Do you have orgies? No, I know: You're all white slaves. You're a colony of artists. This is some funky yuppie commune, right?" At this we both laugh, and she drains my drink.

I take up the empty glass. "Double Felix has a remarkably good instinct about whom he invites to stick around," I say. "Normally it's a matter kept between him and his guest, and only rarely have I suspected anyone of taking advantage. Double Felix is very smart, very special. I have a lot of respect for him. He doesn't care that he supports the people that stay here. To tell you the truth, I doubt he even recognizes that this is a patronal situation, or if he does, he never has bothered to address it as such. As far as what we have here goes, it probably isn't as close as you might think. He and I are close, of course, and there have been other relationships centered around the house, but on the other hand there have been many people who have stayed here that I didn't like and who didn't like me. There have been people living here whose names I never even learned. Remember also that you came here during a party. It can get pretty quiet around here. After all, right now it's just Double Felix, you, me, Zipper, Maggie, and Timmy. There's an empty room, and I've become a virtual recluse. No, there's definitely nothing here to write *Penthouse* magazine about." I hold up my empty glass. "More?" I ask.

Laurie now wears a doubtful smirk. "I haven't had much chance to talk to Felix—Double Felix—since I've been here. He's been staying in his room most of the time. At least I think he's in there. No one answered when I knocked."

The point, finally. "He likes his privacy. I'll tell him you want to talk with him when I see him in the morning—we always have breakfast together. But he'll probably corner you tonight. It's still early. Can I make us another drink?" Fat chance, evidently I'm merely the conduit here.

"No, I can't. That guy Timmy ordered some food, and I promised I'd drive down with him to pick it up. He's a pretty funny guy." She enjoys playing this card; her knee even stopped as she said it.

"Yeah, Timmy's all right. I don't really know him that well, though. Have fun," I say, as I rise to remake my drink. I'm being a brat now; hopefully she'll be flattered.

"Take it easy, William," she says. Old hand. "I'll see you later." This last whispered in my ear during a conciliatory cheek kiss.

And the gin flows as Laurie leaves the deck. The next time I look at my watch it is ten fifteen p.m.

Very cold. Two thirty, it will get colder still. I have awakened with a rare—considering my gin intake lately—desire to urinate. If I go inside at this point, I will probably not be able to bring myself back out. This happened once before: inside for a leak, tempted and lost to my bed, inexplicable guilt for the whole day. No. At this late date—and it must truly be exactly that—I'd rather not risk it. Shivering, I get up to urinate on some weeds that lie on the other side of the railing. Small dribble hits the deck, a false alarm, bladder bluff. Water would be nice; I opt for more gin instead.

With the calendar now firmly rooted in the ambivalence of autumn, sleeping on the deck is much more to the point. A few months ago, as I lay watching fireworks launched from passing yachts, it seemed a fun way to get a little attention, warm nights and pretty stars the only things on and above the horizon. It has since dug itself in, lies deeper, nearer its origin. Now I find I am here for reasons that I can no more control than I can understand.

Closing time. A neon sign blinks for the last time of the night in front of a bar that stands off a small road that runs off the Pacific Coast Highway. Its unnatural blue color makes it one of the more eye-catching elements of the landlocked part of our view. I remember watching my car down there, just sitting in the lot every day for over a month. Then one day I looked and it was gone; they'd finally gotten around to towing it. I couldn't believe how they put up with it for so long. I remember leaving it there. This was my thirty-fourth birthday—I'm now pushing thirty-six—and we had all gone down for a celebration at the bar. Everyone was excited at the chance to actually pay for liquor, and so got very drunk very fast. Refusing to allow myself or anyone else to drive back to the house, I arranged instead for two cabs. The next morning while laughing over our hangover drinks we spotted my car from the deck. Double Felix, glad we'd had a good time, wanted to send me down for it in a limo, but I turned to him and said I really didn't want to leave the house that day and not to worry about the car. I remember him squinting momentarily, smiling and turning away. He stayed out of sight until the following morning when he came into my room at five a.m. and invited me to have vodka with him on his balcony. By the time I noticed that my car had disappeared, Morning Vodka had become a regular conversation hour for him and me, though my car's probable disposition never did come up as a topic. Since then I haven't missed a single hour of vodka with Double Felix, nor any of the other twenty-three as a guest in his house each day.

A quick and distant *crack-crack* tells me I will soon be hearing the far-off flutter of a Los Angeles police helicopter, too far, too late. I don't care; it's too cold to sleep out here anyway. Laurie is haunting my mind. Perhaps I'll find some inspirational warmth hidden under the increasingly unwholesome scenarios that play out behind my eyes and feature her oh-so-supple body. Unlike the other girls I have encountered here over the years, she is, despite her questions, somehow on target. There is a comfortable quality to her demeanor that I've never seen in a new guest, and I can't help but think she has something to teach me. I must also suspect that she will be none too popular with Maggie and Zipper, as they are now feeling quite established and will no doubt resent the more nubile competition. The fact that they, themselves, are both quite attractive will only exacerbate the situation. But this is perhaps as it should be.

Much like Laurie, though I think with different intentions, Maggie simply stuck around after one of the larger parties. This was about six months ago, and unlike with Laurie, Double Felix nailed Maggie immediately. I'm certain that this eventuality was part of her plan, for I had seen her at an earlier party quite aroused, intoxicated, piqued and piquant as she sampled her surroundings and conducted her investigations in a state of wonderment. Halfway through the evening of that previous party I remember seeing her in the back of an empty guest room, hastily removing her bra and panties and putting them in her purse. She now denies this; indeed, Maggie claims she had never been here prior to the party that left her here, claims I must be confusing her with one of Double Felix's call girls—this last, a jab at Zipper. She has come up, as do all guests, in conversation during Morning Vodka. Regarding Maggie, Double Felix was his usual insouciant self.

"William," he said, "why would anyone question the intentions of five foot nine inch redhead? How could you malign a girl with breasts like hers? Who cares if she's lying or whoring or stealing? Just look at her!" Of course, there's just no reasoning with Double Felix when he's been drinking, so I dropped it right there, as I always do.

Zipper Allele is quite a different story, even antithetic to Maggie, and her mention here is admittedly overdue. Inexcusable, my need for and treatment of her is, but not without what I perceive to be a mutual agreement. In fact, Zipper and I are nothing if not in harmony. We are

close to the point of . . . what? Homogeny? I don't know. I do know that
I find it awkward to address her by name, and she me; it feels redundant
somehow, or obvious, overly formal. When I don't know where she is I
panic, but as long as I know she is safe and nearby I feel cocky, like my
time would be better spent elsewhere, doing dirt and building confes-
sions so that I might later beg her soft understanding. Our relationship,
such as it is, I suppose would be called open if it were conducted outside these premises. To me though that label is presumptuous, assuming
talks and treaties that haven't even come close to actually occurring.
We simply never got around to altering our lives except to include each
other in them. Thus the context of what we have to date is exactly
here, firmly rooted in this house; it is here where we met. But unlike
me, Zipper won't be here forever. She of course has a real life and is
reluctant to unite herself completely with the hotbed of inactivity that
is mine. She has a future, a concept too painful for me to consider, and
she has a past, of which I know surprisingly little.

Petite, dark-haired, a hopelessly complex amalgamation of Third
World gene pooling, Zipper came to us through a phone call over a year
ago. I was reading on the deck one afternoon when Double Felix stuck
his head out the door and said, "William, there you are. I've called a
service in Hollywood and asked them to send out a girl. She should be
here around four o'clock. Feel free to come to my room and get a look
at her—say around five or so. If you're interested, I'll pay her extra." I
remember feeling somewhat cranky that day, so though I thanked him,
I had no intention of following through. Eventually, though, I grew inexplicably compunctious about not playing my part and went to knock
on his door. The girl, Zipper, was already on her way out, but armed
with Double Felix's money clip, I was able to persuade her to stay the
evening, and we repaired to my room.

Almost immediately on that first evening our professional relationship began and ended; our personal relationship began and remains.
This has happened to me only once before with a prostitute—and I
have been with many prostitutes. It's like falling for a girl in the super-
market or the library, except that you're already in bed together. The
whole situation was enormously exciting for both of us, highly unusual
and unexpected. The blunt basis of our meeting served as a catalyst
to heighten our sensibilities, and together we saw a clear path that led
straight to the core of what we both then wanted. Zipper was ready for
a break in her life and so made the final call into her service, promising
to stop by the next day with their commission, and we slept well, side
by side.

Looking silently surprised the next morning as he refilled my tum-
bler with chilled Polish vodka, Double Felix met my gaze and awaited
further details. He was uncharacteristically skeptical, possibly jealous,
but ultimately and predictably agreeable. That morning I formally invited Zipper to stay at the house. The next day she returned with her
suitcase. I, of course, with my Midas touch, had her running scared
from my bed and established in her own room by the end of the week.
But, more than even Double Felix, she has accepted my need for distance, and she and I have found a truly friendly groove of congenial de-
pendence laced with very occasional sex. It has been many weeks since
I've slept with Zipper, longer since I've really talked to her, but, oh, how
I dread the hours that she spends away from this house.

The sharp sound of breaking glass awakens me. As I dozed my drink
fell from my hand, rolling for seconds? Hours? It has apparently left the
deck and shattered on one of the many large rocks that lie just over
the edge. The sky may or may not be lighter. Looking west at this hour

requires imagination, which then steals the show. Consulting my watch, I find that I have just under an hour until Morning Vodka, so I pour a short gin in a new glass and wait.

More and more I am emitting the telltale odors of an alcoholic, though I think I have merely the proclivity and not the condition; more and more that seems like a fairly innocuous problem, though I suppose I know better. No matter; without comment Double Felix will tolerate the organically tinged scent of liquor emanating from my pores this morning. He has his own troubles, and I shall shower in lieu of lunch.

I wait here in the very chilly morning. Now I am certain that the sky has grown lighter. I must remember to lean close to Double Felix this morning. Perhaps by now he carries Laurie's redolence on his breath; it would be of fresh air.

CHAPTER TWO

Five to six a.m.: an hour of consistency, of weary, rigid punctuality, a chance to observe the convention of time. Already on the balcony and glancing at his watch as I yawn into his room, Double Felix looks momentarily wistful as if he is about to wax nostalgic, but he never does. Instead, his attention turns to the perennial ice bucket, from which he extracts a bottle of Wódka Wyborowa. A tall man, thin of figure albeit somewhat bloated in detail, his nose might be referred to as Roman; his eyes are very sharp, miss nothing, and he says without looking up, "William, good to see you looking so well rested. But tell me, William, how do you see me looking? Why is it your eyes always linger on my face one beat longer than would keep me at ease?" Then, hearing no immediate response, he says, "Do you understand the question?"

I have crossed the room and now join him at the table on his balcony. "You seem cranky," I say as he fills my glass. "I was hoping to find Laurie here this morning. What's taking you so long?" Actually, I think I'm relieved not to find her here, but I can't help my curiosity. No matter. He, too, chooses not to respond.

Yes, it is definitely morning. The sky is truly lighter than it was earlier. No amount of imagination on my part could account for it; it is a day. It is also still very cold, and Double Felix and I sit, meekly bearing up, shivering silently and awaiting further comment.

Double Felix has one of those faces that seems burdened with ineffable knowledge—or at least observation. Watching him gaze sadly at his vodka, I am struck with the unbecoming desire to be a woman, so that I might be better equipped to comfort and care for him. Though it is doubtful that such an experiment would be satisfying to either of us, the thought no longer frightens me as it surely must have in the past; indeed, I am finding fewer and fewer reasons to draw arbitrary lines around my morals, to declare the perimeter of my behavior.

Determined to push it, and perhaps by way of a wishful and vicarious sacrifice, I say, "It's only that she's such a comely little thing. I would have thought you'd lose no time in sequestering her to your sack." He drains his glass and pours us both more as I continue. "I don't know. Truthfully, the girl appeals to me in a way that is new to me; at least it seems new to me. I'm not sure how to approach her, so I guess I've decided the thing to do is fuck her—for lack of a better idea. But since I'm not having any luck on my own, maybe I was hoping that you would." I stop and, catching his eye for the first time this morning, smile affectionately; I am trying to indicate that what I'm about to say is a mixture of insight and parodic speculation. "Maybe what I really want is to fuck her with your dick. Maybe I'm no longer interested in anything that hasn't first been signed, soiled, or seeded by you." I briefly consider that I may have just regurgitated what I have not yet chewed, but actually, there have been plenty of similar ruminations, and Double Felix smiles broadly at me, almost nodding his head.

"We are indeed tortured men," he says with a chuckle and his glass poised in the air as if to toast our torture. Then, swallowing deeply, "Of course you are correct. She's truly adorable, and I do hope to lure her to my bed," he looks up sharply, "provided that you are not, by then, monopolizing her attentions."

"So what's the problem? Where is she? I've never known you not to be able to lead a girl to your whims."

"What shall I say, William? You overestimate me. Make no mistake: Of course I want to sleep with her, but I no longer feel the urgency that I once did for every pair of panties that walks into the house. Some women should be savored." He momentarily drifts off with that thought. Returning with a surprisingly bitter visage, he says, "Take her if you can, my friend. I don't know what the fuck you expect from me!" But his own petulance is immediately apparent to him, and he softens with, "After all, if I'm not in her pants I'd rather have you in her pants, because, certainly, someone belongs in her pants."

I consider mentioning that Laurie was asking about him—I had told her I would—but now find that I have grown slightly uncomfortable with the conversation; in fact, both Double Felix and I generally avoid this sort of tension, and though I seem lately to have developed a proclivity for discomfort, I prefer to savor it privately. Scanning the Pacific Ocean, half expecting it to reveal to me some pressing matter of conversational urgency, I decide instead not so much to change the subject as to merely move it off center.

"That's a fairly sexist remark," I say (like this is news).

But he decides to pick it up, and says, "Come now, I don't think that you really believe that. The only real sexism is misogyny, and there's none of that in this room."

"Double Felix, you're saying that the two words are synonymous. I don't think you really believe that."

"Maybe not, William. It's all a mystery to me: abstruse codes of conduct and speech, so many pretty painted toes threatening to fall underfoot. There's an element of uncertainty in dealing with these independent women. It's analogous to the inability of many well-intentioned white men to comfortably relate to blacks; there's too much history yet to be overcome; we can't discern the justice/revenge ratio that we know must be lurking behind these new forces that we're dealing with. William, you know perhaps better than anyone that I harbor no ill will toward any woman or man. Faced with an enigma such as this, I can only retreat to kindness. I daresay that the concept of sexism truly does not exist in the context of this house. Hell, it's like a goddamn Third World coup—this is a battle that we can safely ignore; it simply doesn't belong here."

Of course, there is no disputing his anomalous logic. I am once again placed in awe of his acute self-awareness, and I indicate my deference with an empty glass at the end of an outstretched arm.

As Double Felix pours more vodka, I say, "Why don't you marry Zipper? You two deserve each other." This is intended to be adulatory, and because he knows Zipper, knows what she means to me, Double Felix takes it that way.

"Don't go offering up your best girl to every half-ass sophist that you meet; it'll piss her off," he says, smiling warmly: the self-deprecating sire. "You're just thrilled to glean another night's worth of justification for your wanton ways."

We often engage in just this sort of banter, and while I am no match for Double Felix, I do suspect that I provide him with whatever he needs to construct these diversions. Now, as he sits smiling, his mind occupied with an up-and-coming pun or some whimsical prolixity, I see that the pain, which perennially clouds his eyes, has abated ever so slightly; the tension has fled his brow, and hand, as it falls absently from the glass and travels to join its counterpart in his lap. I delight in these moments; I feel that I have earned my keep. I see here the essence of his efforts, the very driver, survivalist pilot, of his soul. This little repartee, symbolic microcosm of the milieu he has brought forth, sings more of vitality than verbosity. I am looking at a man doing whatever he needs to do in order to make his life an acceptable premise, that is, to persevere.

And I hope for him that this great toy—this house, the parties, his girls—is enough. I hope that he has found in this what he so clearly sought: a momentary diversion. For I am convinced that, given the moral inferno that quietly eats at his spirit, this is the purest construction he can ever achieve.

Reaching again for his glass, his hand closes, and—I'm sure he is quite unaware of this—his eyes tighten, as they have taken to doing lately every time his attention is drawn back to his vodka. Yes, I believe that the tiny little tics and twitches which inhabit his—any person's—face have become harbingers of a clear and present fuck-up which hasn't yet been apprehended by his mind. More than anyone else I've ever met, Double Felix can drink. He drinks constantly. Of course, it shows in his face, and I have seen him tremble on rare occasions of semi-sobriety, but Double Felix is apparently one of those lucky, very few who can drink copiously for ever and ever; either that, or he has found it to be a more benign diversion than some heretofore undisclosed other private hell, for a man like Double Felix simply could not exist without at least one private hell. But there are chemical, physical, and medical truths that ultimately demand attention, distant though they may be for some, and I fear that this idiosyncratic tightening of the corners of his eyes portends an increasingly rougher road for a man who not only needs, but probably deserves, his tenacious alcoholism.

Suddenly I'm feeling very quixotic; I want to take a bullet—or some such nonsense—for the man seated before me; I want to paint for him a picture of his own significance. So, with what I have come to believe will be my lifelong immaturity, I become my own decrier, a role that often beguiles the weak. Rubbing my eyes—theatrics for us both—I say, "C'mon, Double Felix, Zipper's ten times the woman that I'll ever be. She outgrew me about two minutes after we met. These days I'm just a piece of patio furniture anyway. You should seriously think about spending more time with her." I can see he is getting bored with this; so am I. Time to move along, but unable to leave the earlier question alone, I add, "After all, you do have all that free space in your bed. Right?" This produces a very fleeting, but nonetheless intense, look of fury on Double Felix's face. He catches it, kills it, then follows through with the instinctive vodka reach.

No comment.

"Laurie! What!" I shout, throwing my glass over the railing. I have the most remarkable feeling of insanity: the moment splits; now it is just an unlikely memory. Double Felix remains impassive, but I see him. So obvious, I feel quite the fool for having never made him. He is a drunk because it is a hell that can be purchased; it's a fix. The quest for alcoholism itself is a fix. Oh, surely by now he has acquired the actual addiction, but that is merely a side effect of his self-prescribed treatment. Unless I am very wrong, alcohol is the least of his problems. I quickly reach for a new glass and fill it, then another.

Without any reference to my inexplicable outburst (I wonder if he even noticed) he says with alarming perception, "You know, William, I stopped drinking once for about two years. This was quite some time ago, long before I lived here." At this point Double Felix dips his right hand, as much as will fit, into his glass. Pulling it out, he splashes his face in the manner, I suppose, of a one-armed man over a washbasin. "When I resumed, which I did utterly intentionally, I found that I had forgotten how." He looks at me. "Forgotten how to drink," he says.

Then, looking off over the water: "Oh, quantity was no problem; I was up to speed in no time. What I mean is that I forgot what to drink when—is this at all clear?—I reverted to what I used to call an amateur status, if that was possible, considering that the entire episode occurred way before I understood quality drinking."

He falls silent, so trying now to make him smile, I tell him, "Sounds great, Double Felix. The sacramentalist sheep in AA would have a field day with that. I can hear them now, all paroxysmal, choked with vision, each racing to be the first to spit the word *denial* at your little lost face while the remainder pull back fast, lest they appear discordant, and nod in solemn unanimity."

And he does smile, saying, "They are a rather zealous bunch, aren't they? Certainly more conniving than most people suspect, probably more chicaning than even they know."

I want to ask him what chicaning means, but I can see that he wishes to expand further on his drinking.

Pouring more vodka, he says, "Some of the happiest moments in my life have been spent yakking away under the influence, blabbing to some new acquaintance about nothing in particular. The alcohol was then a medicine, quelling for a time whatever it is in me that keeps me isolated within myself, and allowing me to really enjoy talking with other people. I'm not sure I ever understood my solitude. I worry if it—I can't think of the word—I worry that maybe it has something to do with my leading everything to the wrong place."

He looks to me—for what? A word? An answer? I am lost. There was a time when I would have feigned acumen and laid down some sort of specious verbal shuffle in an effort to reaffirm my value. Now I simply say, "I'm sorry, Double Felix, I don't understand."

With a twitch and a startled look, he suddenly jumps from his chair and enters his room. Returning a moment later, he extracts the half-full vodka bottle from the ice bucket and replaces it with a new one, its seal still unbroken. Then, after topping off my glass, he walks to the far end of the balcony, where he drinks off the rest of the first bottle. This done, he asks me, "So William, do you think we ought to put together a little party for tonight?"

But he's not really interested in my answer. He's just waiting for the Wódka Wyborowa to give him his morning fuck, after which his voice will take on a subtle breathiness that no one but me seems to notice, and he will speak only of things that he wishes to.

"Oh, you shouldn't worry, Double Felix. No doubt your good friend Maggie is even now composing in her dreams a guest list with which she can surprise you later. You know, two or three small clusters of people, destined to be identified only by nicknames as she shows them around her crash, and vaguely connected with some promising film project that's 'gonna be huge,' or perhaps a series that's 'slated for the new season,' an album about to be recorded because 'the guys are ready to go into the studio.' Have you ever noticed that her friends are all low-mileage people who are nevertheless obsessed with turning back their odometers?"

He spins. I have given him his voice. "Dog!" he spits in mock outrage. "Decrier of goddesses!" Having regained his humor at this oft-repeated joke, he regains, also, his chair, and says in a voice that rings with true affection, "William, I think it's been far too long since I've done you a favor. How would you like me to evict Maggie? We could load up her room with a new girlfriend for you. We'll manufacture your whole past and make her think that you're the one with all the money. You'll be married and living in Santa Barbara in no time. I'll co-vertly send you checks and whatever else it takes to provide the illusion that you're completely immersed in the world of commerce. Yes, yes. How 'bout it? It'll be great. We'll get you an office in Beverly Hills and you can spend the weekdays there—ostensibly, of course. You'll really come and stay here with me all week and drive up to Santa Barbara on the weekends to revel in bliss with your diamond-clad, poolboy-fucked wife." He sits back, satisfied.

No response is required; we both know how stupid this is, though I suppose it could be started—would be started if he thought for a moment that it was what I wanted. What really disturbs me is his initial offer to bounce Maggie. Not that I would care, but to say something like that, even in the context of a joke, is so unlike Double Felix, so alien to everything I know about him, that it immediately disorients me. In fact, the idea of Double Felix actually being mean to somebody is discomforting to the point of making me want to rush from the balcony. More than all the other odd indications and strange subcurrents that are running through his space this morning, this gives me real cause to believe that something is not as it should be, at least not as it has been.

"Tell me about the come," I say.

"What come are you referring to?"

"Remember the other night in the big room? I was talking to that black kid with the UCLA shirt, and you came up behind me and whispered in my ear: *Ask me about come tomorrow morning.* I had forgotten it until just now. So, tell me what you meant." Double Felix is forever getting notions about anything and everything, and when he does, he invariably pulls me aside and asks me to inquire later about whatever it is he is thinking. I normally never do, thinking that it will all be covered in the course of conversation anyway, but this one popped into my head just when I needed a diversion: more quick maintenance for my increasingly neurotic personality.

"Ah, yes, I remember. I was talking to one of those waitresses that always seem to show up from the restaurant down the hill. She was complaining to whoever would listen about her boyfriend. Apparently he has a penchant for his own semen; he likes to touch and taste it. The girl—Sandy or Cindy, I think—finds this behavior to be strictly odious; in other words, it doesn't quite fit her teen-rooted decoupage of masculinity, but as she so eloquently balanced her quandary: 'He's like . . . HUNG. I mean he's way hung. No way I'm walkin' on that!' When she told me that, I had to laugh. It reminded me of the joke about the two old women bemoaning the quality of the food served in the restaurant they frequent: . . . *and such small portions.* Anyway, the scene is that SandyCindy has to suck him dry—but he won't let her swallow it—and then spit and lick it all over his face, eventually scooping it with her tongue into his open mouth. He then savors every drop and offers to go down on her, but of course, by then she's too grossed out to enjoy it. So they end up fucking, which I gather is a fairly long process because she claims that he can't come unless they're doing his little oral act. That can't be lost on her either, another mark in the plus column of his scorecard."

We chuckle over this, but I know it's merely the prelude to his real point. Entertaining hunting-lodge fare, maybe a shocker for some unsuspecting new arrival, but this is not the type of story that Double Felix relates for its own value. No, there's a point pending. Wait . . . then the mouth cocks, the eyes lock just past my own, searching for the means to push . . . out . . . the . . . next . . . word . . .

"So, after unsuccessfully trying to lure SandyCindy to my room for a more compelling demonstration, I retired there alone and contemplated her boyfriend. I mean, what a genius! What an artist! I love the guy. Buried though it may or may not be, he must have a sublime respect for either himself or life or both. I tried to create in my mind the image of SandyCindy, a disdainful look smeared across her face, taking up the white girl's burden and following selflessly her master's voice as it issues from her little corner of whoredom. There he would lie, blissful, perhaps ignorant of a stray drop taking refuge behind his earlobe, or a forgotten string running between SandyCindy's molars and flashing only briefly as she opens her mouth to whine. It occurred to me that semen has precisely the most appropriate, the most seemly physical properties for what it is: life-provoking spermodial ooze, pungent, racy, attractive and repellent to the men and the boys. He's tapped into his own fountain of truth. He's an addict, a self-serving, self-fucking, kinky come-eater, thinks he's discovered perpetual commotion. Poor little SandyCindy was predisposed to eschew not the come, but her boyfriend's acceptance of it. She lost her chance to dig it in some long forgotten schoolyard, when she finally did something or other for the simple reason that everyone else was doing it. But not him. No, he's a real comer. He takes it with his morning coffee, gets out of bed, washes his face, and seizes the day. Then he puts in his hours, brings home more bread to SandyCindy, and thus gets her to spit more of his own come in his face." Double Felix gives me his eureka! look, and I have to smile; I'm right with him on this one. "The guy's a fucking poet. Hell, I'd drink his come."

"What a shot!" I say, amidst our vodka-stoked guffaws. "What a shot that guy has taken." But Double Felix looks at me quizzically through his laughter—only for a moment—then nods in feckless agreement. In fact, even I don't know what my words mean. Lately I have taken to speech without forethought, often without memory. It all pours with my liquor. It's part of me, and I suppose I like it. Between mutant chuckles: "That reminds me of that stupid story you hear as a kid, the one about the guy in the movie theater who has to hide his boner from his date by pushing it up through the bottom of his popcorn container." At this we both break up again.

"Why the hell are you reminded of that, William? I don't see the connection."

"I don't know. I guess I have the feeling that we've both been had by SandyCindy." We laugh more, comfortable again in our mutual ability to entertain, to provide for ourselves at least that warmth, though I cannot guess to what degree we remain ourselves.

And this is the only game in town. This surely must be, must by now have become, the only game in town. No amount of disconsideration on my part is going to make that an unfact. I cannot think of the future, or the past. They do not exist from where I'm lying.

I feel, though, that things are slipping, that a complex Boy Scout knot has been earnestly configured by some not-so-complex boys. The diagrams in the handbook having been followed carefully, it is now time to pull the ends and check the integrity of the work, and it's starting to look like there's no reason to believe that the knot will hold. I remember as a teenager in high school I got into the habit of eating my sandwich—which, my mother's suspicions notwithstanding, I always insisted on making myself—while taking a brisk walk outside the prescribed perimeters of school property and good studentdom. It sticks in my mind as my first real sense of freedom. Oblique, yes, but that special feeling of simultaneously walking and eating was the nearest I've ever come to experiencing independence. I suppose that within the implied contextual limits that we all must deal with, this is merely what I have chosen to be my symbol, or my source. I only know now that I hope dearly for the endurance of that feeling, and my ability to recapture with ease what has gone to so deep a slumber.

Doubting? Am I doubting my inclination to stay on good terms with this . . . this purchased lawlessness? And what does that mean? Why would such a simplistic, stab-in-the-dark term come dribbling from my brain? There is a constant hum, a haunting of my content, with me, I think, since day one (or day two). Like the guilty discomfort of the alcoholic as he drifts to and from drinks, I have a parasitical notion clinging to my spine. I know not what it is, have faith in neither my comprehension nor my mastery of it. What may be worse: I don't feel up to it.

As he drinks, Double Felix tends to rock in his chair in increasingly acrobatic ways. So when, still reverberating with the remnants of our laughter, he attempts to rise from his chair, he finds himself temporarily trapped by an unaccounted for mingling of chair leg and table leg. Naturally, he reacts slowly and in a manner that is less than helpful to his predicament, causing himself to topple, and tugging the table just enough to unseat my elbow, which leads to my hand, which dumps my colder-than-it-ought-to-have-been drink into my lap. My testicles tell me it is time to jump up, and my legs take the order before my brain can countermand it. I go left and down. Double Felix is already getting comfortable on his back as I land. The table, teetering for what seems like an eternity, finally joins us with a crash to rival the best-staged sound effect.

Choking with laughter, we are in our element. I suddenly feel competent, good at what I do. These absolutely humiliating moments of classic drunk are a source of endless amusement and comfort to me, and to Double Felix as well.

"Christ," Double Felix manages through slapstick tears, his face sanguine and overcome with hilarity, "are you hurt, William?"

"No. You?" I respond, barely audibly. But we surrender again to our hysterics, and I don't get an answer. Eventually I kick away my chair and lie flat on my back. Double Felix is reaching around haphazardly with both hands, then the legs too. "I got it," I say, my fingers finding and closing around the familiar shape of a vodka bottle. Horizontal, it has only drained to the level of its neck. I take a drink and roll it over to him.

"Thank you," he says. We are now both comfortable again, albeit still on the ground. Like the vodka, we have successfully sought our own level and are now preparing to resume our conversation.

"I can't believe how much fun that was," I say. "We haven't done that for too long."

"What? Fallen off of our chairs? Are you suggesting that this is something we should undertake with regularity? I'm sorry, William, but I think that premeditation would have tainted the moment—at least in this case."

Lying contentedly on the hard surface of the balcony and looking at the brightening sky, we are enjoying a refreshing perspective on gravity. The words, whatever they may be, feel fresh and worth pronouncing as they endeavor to rise from my mouth and throat in untrained ways. Something familiar has awakened just behind my eyes and wants to continue the journey. A gentle but insistent tug to the ever more deeply quartered places, perhaps an ancient disdain for uprightness, beckons me southward.

"So what are you doing today?" I ask.

He giggles, repeating the question under his breath in subtle confirmation. "What would inspire you to ask such a thing, William? You know that is a question I have never felt obliged to answer. Hell, you know that I couldn't answer it—couldn't answer it to save my life. Never've been able to." I can feel him turning his head to look at me. With a laugh: "How is your day shaping up? Got anything slated? A lunch? Perhaps a two o'clock?"

Trammeled, remembering that he and I used to joke with these very absurdities back when we first started meeting for Morning Vodka, I pick up his laughter. "Well no, actually. It turns out that I'm all clear today. I though we might break with tradition and spend the day drinking together out here. I'm parched."

I turn, waiting for his volley, but his face is now distracted and somewhat darker. "Sorry, William," he says, "but I'm afraid not. It's really not a good time for me to be recklessly breaking traditions." He sits up, then rises fully and commences to right the table.

My motion to assist is halted with a flash of his palm, but I stand just the same and walk to the railing where I watch the water and wonder how I managed to dampen things.

"William," he says, "why don't you have a nice talk with Laurie today. After all, she is recently arrived from the outside world. Perhaps she could bring you up-to-date." Then, more pointedly: "You have been away for a while. Isolated. I understand that the universe has been found to vibrate in a most harmonious way, and South Central L.A. is a battle zone. Go ahead; get the latest dope from our newly arrived wire servicer. Your cave won't be far."

Aghast and injured, I feel my frame literally sag under the weight of this unprecedented and inexplicable spleen. "It's almost six," I say, turning to leave through his room in an attempt to regain my orientation.

Double Felix is suddenly, unsteadily in front of me. Wavering as he blocks my exit, he must have risked limb and much balance to cross the balcony that quickly, this drunkenly. "I—stop for a second—William."

This unusual verbal misfire catches my attention, coming as it does from a man who is always eloquent. Perhaps just another puzzle piece, perhaps the one that fits with the uncharacteristic cruelty, it is the one that makes me stop and listen.

He continues, "An apology seems somewhat trite, though I freely

offer one. You have seen that I am distracted. Please take it as merely
that. I suppose that my house of cards has fallen into disarray, temporarily. I don't know. Try to understand that this is a matter that I must deal
with inwardly." I start to speak, but he stops me with a gesture and says,
"You want to offer your support and help. I know that I have them, and
if there was some assistance I felt you could render, I would consider its
availability a forgone conclusion." He gains a righted chair, and now
seated, looks up at me. "This . . . anomaly," he says doubtfully, "is not
threatening my health or wealth . . . or anything."

A sudden broad smile and an abrupt leap for more vodka lead me to
say, "You're gay, right? You want to fuck every deep voice in a twenty-mile
radius—starting with me—and you just can't handle it. You've gone
crazy sending checks to Oral Roberts, but it only seems to get worse
every time you write his name. Nothing seems to help, so you've decided to alienate everyone you know as the most nonphysical form of
self-abuse you can think of."

"Don't be absurd," he says. "We've always known that I'm gay.
You're the one that would find Jesus hiding behind that little piece of
self-discovery."

We both laugh the overly enthusiastic laughter of relief, and it feels
good to not address our distress.

Double Felix looks right at me and allows a beat to indicate that
what he is about to say is of some importance to him. "William, what do
you suppose is the difference between want and need? It occurs to me
that whenever the two converge there is a penance due."

"Due whom?"

"Oh, whoever observes right and wrong; oneself; the aggregate of
goodness; the concepts of love and humility; the point which lies furthest from dogma."

"Don't you think the idea of a penance is, in itself, rather dogmatic?"

He is expecting this, but instead of a lengthy oration, he simply says, "No, only in the context of religious sophism."

For a long time we say nothing, preferring instead to watch the ocean. Finally breaking the silence, I say, "I think you're not considering a third element."

"What is that?"

"How could one assume responsibility for the simple merging of requirement and desire? I would think the penance would be beside the point, by definition: after the fact. But, more to the point, if a thing is truly required, truly a need, then its procurement is beyond your control, given that your first duty is to continue living."

"Well then," he responds, "you're saying that anything goes. And if the difference between want and need is purely a matter of one's perception, what then?" He blinks at me. "The whim justifies the means? Surely you, William, surely you of all people can do better than that."

"You're too demanding," I say. "No one has—or even should have—the ability to draw distinct borders like that. It's way past us; you can only make an effort."

"Wrong," he says. "Wrong."

It is now past six, and the sun is indisputably up. Squeezing his shoulder, I take my solicitous leave.

CHAPTER THREE

Walking from Double Felix's closed door, I hear a car pull up to the house. It is Laurie and . . . Timmy. Well, that takes care of that. Salty come, probably from eating too many Beer Nuts, and Christ, what a vocabulary. When's the last time I heard the term blow job? I must have been in high school. I just hope he's not in love. I don't know; this was a bit much. Maybe I should have stayed up here talking with William. In any case, I'm gonna have to start coming up with better ways to spend the night. You know you're in trouble when you start sleeping with guys named Timmy . . . you sorry motherfucker. Damn if there aren't one or two things I did with her that I wouldn't do with most girls! Fuck! Most girls don't have nice hard tits like that. Boy, did she stand out like a fucking picture or what? What the fuck kind of luck do I have, anyway? Best piece of ass I ever got, and no one to tell about it. This place is driving me nuts. What a crime. I gotta get back to my friends.

Too bad she didn't go for the backseat. It would have been kind of cold, I suppose, but I can stand a little chill if it means saving forty bucks. But what the fuck, who am I to complain? I guess I've spent a lot more than forty on dinners that never even panned out, let alone pay dirt like Laurie. Sometimes it just pays to go along with what they want and make them feel like they're in charge. I just don't see why we couldn't do it here at the house. I don't see what her problem was with that idea. Then, to top it all off, she wants to come right back up here at six in the fucking morning. What gives? She won't fuck up here, but she won't stay and sleep down there.

I suppose the best-looking ones are always quirky. Like that secretary, that Janice girl, that temp from last year. Nicest fucking body you could ever wish for, but just don't let her open her mouth! I remember her last day: Fucking Chase takes her out for lunch cause he was in Cayman for Harper's fat-fuck what's-his-name mini-mall client, and no one ever cued him on how fucked-up she was. Fucking Chase! Fucking anything-that-moves Chase. Has dinner with her, listens to her yap all night, and still nails her! I guess he thought he earned it. Hell, he did earn it, but I wouldn't have done her. Especially not after she almost made that little scene in the file room, no way I'd do her after that. Fucking Chase goes home in the middle of the night, and his wife wants to know why his mustache smells like pussy. Oh fuck! We all fucking died over that, laughing our asses off, Hoop-man at the sink, trying to eat his lunch and cracking up, food falling out his mouth and soda coming out his nose. What a fucking riot. I miss those guys. I could go back. I bet they meant it when they said I could come back. Plenty of litigation to go around. I should go back. This place is dead. Bill would never get a story like that, not like Chase. Fucking Chase! Bill's a deadbeat. I should go back.

Felix. What a setup Felix has here. Strange fucker, but still a nice guy. I mean, who am I to complain? No sir, I'm not complaining, not after a four-month free ride. No way am I complaining. It's just that these guys seem to have no backbone. Bill could be poppin' his live-in hooker every night if he wanted; instead he just sits out on that patio jacking off. And Felix does get a good share of ass, but they make him look bad, the way he lets them take advantage and walk all over him. I've even seen him be nice and smile to some son of a bitch that just got done insulting him. Hell, anybody fucks with me and I turn their lights out. That's self-respect. That's what Felix needs. I swear I don't know where that guy is coming from.

But man, if I had a setup like this, no way would I turn it over to a bunch of strangers. This chick Laurie, for instance, nice fuck, sure, but does Felix even know that? I doubt it. No, she could be anybody. Just waltz in and stay for as long as you like. For all he knows she could be here to rip him off. Yeah, if this was my place you wouldn't see anybody but my friends hanging around, and maybe some chicks, but not just anybody. And you sure wouldn't find me hiding in my room, no fucking way. I would be right out with my buddies, all the livelong day, and we would parrr-teeee!

Of course, Laurie could be there anytime she wanted, now that I know her. Any chick that sucks dick the way she does definitely gets to drink my beer. Good listener too. Actually, I'm sort of surprised that I knocked her at all. Not that I'm not able to get all I need; I never have to pay for it or anything like some guys do, like that story Walt-n-chips told about when he was in Atlanta for Floratron and paid twenty bucks for a blow job—from a black chick, no less. Fucking Walt-n-chips. Or like Bill, probably. I bet old my-name's-william Bill has shelled out some green in his time. Laurie's out of his league anyway, more my speed. It's just that Laurie didn't seem too interested, really just friendly sort of. Then, before I knew it, she's got me reaching between her legs. She just sort of sighed like she was good and ready and let me go ahead. Until, that is, I tried to pull my dick out of my pants. Next thing I knew I was shelling out forty bucks for a room. She sure is in good shape, though. She has that way that some chicks have of being able to move every muscle. In fact, for a while it seemed like she was trying to take charge, sort of fighting me with her legs. I figured, what the hell? Let her have her little ego trip. I knew that I could make her stutter and turn dumb if I really wanted to. Or, well, whatever. I don't really mean to say bad stuff about her—she's pretty cool for a chick—but next time I'll have her singing a different tune. Hell, she was probably getting worried about being stuck with the deadbeat squad here at the house, and now she's thrilled at finding someone who can keep up with her. Probably just putting me through the paces to make sure she wasn't dreaming. Probably that's it.

I bet a girl like Laurie would kill a guy like Bill. She's so much more than he could handle. Chase could tag her, even Hoop-man or Gibson, even fucking Walt-n-chips could probably handle that, probably if me and Chase coached him from the fucking sidelines, but a guy like Bill would never be able to figure out what to do with all that supercharged pussy. But so what? I mean, hell, I guess he's an okay guy. I just feel sorry for him sometimes. But then, I'm not about to go around being depressed over people that just don't get it. Fuck 'em. Sink or swim. Nothing's that hard.

CHAPTER FOUR

. . . Timmy, evidently just now returning from their alleged food expedition. Things must have gotten trysted around. I was right to be cranky to Laurie last night on the deck, but rather than stand here and embarrass myself with some sort of wanna-be-a-cuckold fantasy, I go on down the hall and slip silently into Zipper's room.

Zipper Allele, unlike me, is not in the habit of policing the area at six-oh-something a.m. Rather, she sleeps easily through the up-and-coming buzz of the morning; this I have oft observed, silent hours on the floor next to her bed spent in worship at an alter of cotton, a futon of unsprung wait. Her voluminous black hair dominates a white down pillow that would appear oversized in any other context. She is, under the fluff of her sheets and covers, naked and alive. Perceptive—or should I say sensitive?—to a keen degree, she will know, even in her sleep, that I am in her room. I've seen this before: motionless, then her nose briefly twitches. She has my scent, eau de Caucasian drunk deadbeat, and without waking, she shifts, clears my place, waits patiently for what warmth I have to offer. So far, this has proved to be the best antidote in my life, to my life. How I wish I could have her cinnamon skin; how I wish I too could be unfathomable to the powers that be. I wish I could be of her race, the not-white race, and so be despised and feared by my vapid brethren without working so damn hard at it. She is on the far side of her bed. I know there is a space for me under her sheet, but I lie above the cover instead and feel what I can of her.

Now the sounds of the house—Laurie and Timmy coming in, conspicuous in their whispers—have fallen into the obscurity of that which lies outside of Zipper's door. Even the two sets of footfalls—I think, yes, diverging—fail to capture my attention. I'm a big boy in a big family. My mom's sleeping naked next to me, and if I should feel the need, I can nuzzle up to her and suckle her breast. That's about the size of it—now disconnected sets of noises definitely from different parts of the house—never mind that in reality it would be far too easy. Our peculiar burden prohibits actual mother fucking, so we must recast our actual mothers before going about our dirty deeds.

Lately I have been giving some thought to the source of Zipper; that is, how she was delivered to me—if, indeed, she was delivered to me, this Sud American slut who has penetrated far more deeply into me than I have into her. Thirty years old, an outcall hooker (a vocation she regards as trite and a bit beside the point, certainly not requiring the hell-and-back shoulder chip worn by most girls lying in that bed) working a third-party telephone trammel which hangs in and above Los Angeles, she was suddenly summoned into a strange new world by a callout from Double Felix, followed by the appropriate footnote of an invitation from me, after the fuct, it was. Now here we lie, of the same bed. It is a scene that could very well have existed first in Double Felix's willful imagination, implementation pending arrival of appropriately sympathetic piece of ass. Yes, it would be well within his vision to at least wish for such a thing, that it might help to keep things well. Foreseeing my current state of personal malcontent, he could have deemed it necessary to introduce a new element meant explicitly for me, a gift subscription to a little regular, watchful, maternal affection. Not that he went shopping with those specific requirements, but I do think he may have set in motion more wheels than he normally keeps spinning. I recall meeting a lot of women around that time; he made a lot of bets, and one paid off. Zipper Allele, as unknowingly warded by his intentions as I, showed up in his bed for a test drive. He knew that I'd end up asking for the keys. It all could, perhaps should, bother me, but there is really no good reason for it to. This is Double Felix's realm, and that has always been self-evident to me, regardless of how offhandedly he appears to approach it. He does not venture beyond his walls, does not ask for anything but company, does not ask even that we remember his name. Ultimately, this place is for him. He is the one who needs it.

"You forgot how to lie in the bed," murmurs Zipper, alluding to my contortive, semireclined position. Even in this state she is thick of accent and won't give up her now sleepy, but always choppy and distinctive syllables: You ForGot How To Lie In The Bed. "Finally you have spent so much time sleeping outside that you don't know how to sleep inside anymore."

"Don't be silly. I just can't decide if I want to stick around or not. I'm vacillating."

"You are Vaseline—right? You want to make it easy for everyone to jerk off."

"No, that's Double Felix. And that's crude. You don't talk like that when you're awake. I think I'll come back then." I move to touch between her legs, more out of familiar affection than lust, but she pushes my hand away.

Into her pillow: "You don't mean business. I can tell. If you really want to be useful you'll go find me a real man. Go find me Timmy. I'm ready to give him his way with me."

This makes me wonder if she knows about Timmy and Laurie. Of course she does, but how? They must have talked. Women always tell each other about that sort of thing. But opting not to bring up Laurie, I say, "Oh, has he been bothering you? Do you want me to go out there and set him straight, tell him to stay away from my . . . my girl-that-I-sleep-with-now-and-then-so-don't-nobody-else-fuck-with-her?"

She giggles. "Yeah! Nobody fuck with her! That will be a good day. My man, my provider. You want to keep me chained in the kitchen? If you do, okay. But first go and straighten him out like you said."

Rather than respond I try again to reach under her covers, this time with more conviction, although I'm sure I'm not really up to following through.

"Go ahead," she says, spreading her legs slightly. "You can pretend I'm Laurie." Abruptly closing her thighs, she traps my hand and squeezes. "Now you are pussy whipped," she says, releasing my hand and, presumably, referring to herself. "You will be blind to this, but inside I feel something destructive in her, in Laurie." She turns, now facing me.

I can see that she is ready to be overtly serious, but that is not what grabs my attention. It may be beside her point, but I am again whacked by the sight of her. Before Zipper, I had never known a woman's beauty to deepen daily and unpredictably in my eyes—not past the first few weeks anyway. I wonder if I react visibly at these times. I feel as though I must—sometimes she looks at me a little quizzically—but I've always been afraid to ask; it would sound too stupid to explain, and the whole topic makes me nervous.

Somewhat less distracting, but still not conducive to quiet reflection and studied conversation, are The Colors. They consume my peripheral vision, beyond her face and out of focus, eradicate the basic redundancy of these guest rooms and belie the lily-white consistency so prevalent in the house that Double Felix spilt. The Colors bay and claim their vivid turf. There are bright pink throw pillows thrown onto a lime green comforter and partially covered by a robe only slightly less polychromatic than its owner. Resplendently intricate wall tapestries, abstractly littered with reds, purples, and yellows themselves, litter walls of royally rich blue paper; orange line-drawn, primitive stick figures dance elsewhere on the paper, dance on the blue. There in the corner, a giant papier-mâché piñata of a parrot waits to have its big burnt-burgundy belly burst wide by a haphazard child's swing so that it might finally hemorrhage its sweet booty, sticky Mexican candy and dyed straw toys, a dandy disembowelment—I know, for I have seen one of these go to its fate at a party in the big room, after being reluctantly sacrificed by Zipper. Mobiles, one black bamboo, one multihued tissue paper on a balsa wood frame, a third draped with tiny glass beads, little play prisms, ride on silver picture wire, for now suspended from the powder-blue ceiling. The Colors own the silk kites, outrageous openmouthed fish of nightmarish proportions. The Colors own the towels, thick with rust-red or copper-copper, perfume-grabbing, North Carolina milled cotton, bath sheets, with the occasional musky redolence to prove it. The Colors own the aqua slippers. The Colors own the sunburst socks. The Colors own the emerald in Zipper's ear—still in Zipper's ear; she must have slept with it in, must have forgotten to replace it in her gold jewelry box atop her black lacquer nightstand. And it looks good there, in her ear, not unlike the color of her eyes.

"What do you mean destructive?" I ask, picking up what she has dropped.

More demurely than I would have thought her capable of, she says, "Well . . . she is a very . . . regular? girl [stumbling over a language that we both know she is fluent in], and I think when she came here, she knew already what she would find." Zipper looks at me: Do you get it?

Do you understand the logical leap I am attempting? "People in a place like this are either surprised or surprising. This is a house of cards we are living in."

Impressed with her nuance but still not able to fully grasp her meaning, I blunder with, "You really don't need to feel threatened by her," and the sound of these words pretty much makes me choke.

She dismisses my prattle with a *tsk tsk* which comes off more like a *chiss chiss,* having been Hispanicized in the trickier-than-thou confines of her mouth and forced past those salacious lips. Her countenance briefly assumes a twinkle, as if brightened for a moment for a photographer or a trick. This is Zipper's wisdom rearing its amazing head. She knows something, something about either me or the world. In any case, it applies directly to what we've been discussing, and she will never let me in on it, will never even admit it. Whatever passed behind her eyes, I'm sure she is confident that it will become clear to me with time. I feel at once resentful and randy: If she won't let me in her club, perhaps she'll let me fuck its only member. I don't know. She's some sort of watcher, keeper of an arcane prescient-mystic-hooker force. She's got my number—I don't even have my fucking number—and that may well be the source of our . . . amicable asunderment? For how can I be expected to go steady with a girl who is conversant with my soul? How can I not? This woman seems to have infinite patience, or is that a side effect of perspicacity? I wouldn't know; I have infinite ennui. It only looks like patience, but without the little glow: the waiting for without the for.

Zipper is my pimp. I'm a philosophical bone-digger in love with the dormant verb of my life. I am the passive voice. I vigorously assert it to myself on a constant basis. I mope around, sleep outside, get drunk and wear my little shield of independence and isolation, proud and protected. But with her, between her and me, I give it up on demand—or I used to. Still do, I guess. What this has to do with our relationship, I don't know. If she says it, I do it, and not because I want to. No, I smile for Zipper because it's what I have to do to survive. No room in this bed for integrity of purpose; this bed is only big enough for my stupid grin and Zipper's sublime breasts, hair, pussy, lighthearted weariness. She is sure as hell better than . . .

. . . them. So elemental, they are. So detailed, they are. With their small-world reasoning, their well-timed ticks, and their choppy little once-learned tricks, still better than our best-practiced studies. The hint of an outline of a suggestion of a nipple nestled behind a light-weight poly-cotton blend. A lone stream of sweat bisecting a buttock. A subtle imperfection, perhaps a line around the mouth or a misplaced pound. A stray glance or a stray pubic hair. An unobserved observation of a once-over in a convenient mirror. A tan line. The absence of one. An implication. At their best, that's what they are. An implication. Obsession used to be my M.O., then depression. Now I've given up. A sign of maturity. A taste of success.

Zipper is my simple talk, my savvy chick. Making love to her once, I heard her utter a foreign exclamation. I don't even think she was aware of it; in any case, she claims not to remember, and considering her passion, I believe her. She also claims her great-grandmother was a black slave in Brazil, but this is only one of many such tales I have heard from her, some conflicting. She does have that subtle libidinal superiority that I've felt in black girls. Guiltily, I have even considered her grandmother as a young girl. Coyly concupiscent in her inadequate rag dress, eyes boldly darting from their downward cast, she whimpers as I take her on the straw mattress of her shack, where she silently plots my murder. This is an admittedly odd construction, but my sullied white soul can simply not imagine fucking a black girl and having her not be in control—more of a failure of my imagination than a truth of the world. Maybe my fantasy is allegorical to my failure with Zipper, for unlike her might-have-been murderous ancestress, I can expect no such savage deliverance from her; she does not share my propensity for quixotism. I could make love to her now; that is, she would let me. But I won't, though I think I want to. My penis stiffens with the thought, the vision, but no go. Perhaps it is the milieu that is dysfunctional; perhaps it is me, albeit on some beefier level than mere impotence.

Tossing aside her sheet, she rises from her bed and walks naked to her balcony. At once the drapes and the glass door are thrown open, and I am overwhelmed by a rush of daylight and ocean breeze, somehow warmer now, filtered, as it is, through and by her body.

"Feel how nice it is, and so early. It would be a good day to go to the beach with me," she says. Half turning, she exposes her nakedness in backlit silhouette, as if to illustrate that any day would be a good day to go to the beach with her.

But she knows better. She knows that it has been quite some time since I've gone to the beach with her, or with anyone else, for that matter. By now she must even have a good idea of how fearful I am of the world at large, how unlikely it is that I could leave this house for any reason—an earthquake, a fire, to save my life, much less a walk on the beach. Christ! Last night on the deck I couldn't even manage to piss on the other side of the railing. The railing: the self-imposed perimeter of my activities. The deck: the new frontier. As with all the great men of history, I am compelled to live on the edge. Perhaps that is why I insist on sleeping out there, out in the untamed land of oak and wicker, aluminum and canvas. Yes, that's me: always pushing the envelope. I must look truly ridiculous. Every night when I go out there to my chair and settle in, it's as if I'm ready to have the credits come rolling over my face—music slowly building, the conclusive moment about to play itself out by surrendering theatrically into the black resolution of fade-out, the most effortless of endings.

"No, I think not," I simply say.

Spinning on her heel, she steps out, still naked, onto her balcony, and though this produces quite an effect from where I'm sitting, I know that she is only trying to hide her pout. An incongruity—the point of a pout is demonstrative—it is nonetheless very much something that she, inscrutably, would do. For a moment I feel like a spoiled child who secretly craves discipline but knows that such a thing could never and should never be requested.

"Maybe Timmy and Laurie will go to the beach with me," she says over her shoulder.

"Yeah, good plan! Better yet, you could ask Maggie along. You two would have a blast down there. Besides, with you standing out there like that, it won't be long before the whole of Malibu organizes into a mob and marches up here demanding a closer look at your tits. You could stop all that before it happens." I'm being obnoxious.

She turns again and enters the room, majestic and proud in her nudity, her smile replaced and imploring, her eyes unwavering and insatiable. "Would you like me to stay with you today? I could stay with you here at the house. We could eat lunch outside on my balcony and make love after that. If you want. Or I could go out and run some errands. Is there something you need?"

"No, but buy yourself something on my behalf."

"Very romantic," she says, nesting her copper-tone ass on the floor at the foot of the bed, leaning back against the bed and spreading her hair out in a quick commotion between a practiced neck and hand.

"Now you are talking like a pimp I had at the beginning. He told us to call him Al, but he was an Arab who wore lots of gold jewelry. He had more rings and necklaces and bracelets than anybody else I know. It was years ago, when Hollywood was easy and a lot of girls didn't even have pimps. I was new here and didn't know any better. I only stayed with him for maybe two months. I left when I wasn't his favorite anymore. But when I was still with him, whenever I came home and gave him my money he would give me some back—maybe two or three hundred sometimes. He always said something like that, like: *Go and buy yourself something from me,* or: *Here's for a nice present from Al.* But I left him."

I sit up on the bed and say, "What the hell's that? The fucking Parable of the Pimp? The Allegory of the Arab Ass Trader? I can't tell you how happy I am, after all this time, to hear about how I remind you of your pimp!" I'm doing my best to look upset, though truly I always feel flattered to be told these stories of her past, thrilled with any degree of intimacy. However, as often happens to me, the situation gathers a current beyond my constraint, with the result that Zipper's failure to even witness my indignation completes, in my mind, the snubbing.

"Don't be silly. It's just a story," she yawns, now cursorily checking her nails.

"Damnit! If you're gonna tear me down, at least have the courtesy to look at me." Even as I say this it occurs to me that I talk too much and too quickly. Like a loose-cannon disk jockey juggling a switchboard full of sociopathic callers-in, my show could benefit from the implementation of a tape delay, a verbal loop that could be interrupted on its way out of my mouth.

Stretching catlike, then rising, she says, "It is not me who you are angry with . . ." She pulls her hair behind her head, as women will, and does whatever is done with it at that point. The raising of her arms causes her breasts to lift yet higher, and I imagine even that her hips thrust slightly toward me, as if involved in the effort. ". . . is it?" She lets her arms fall, abandoning her hair, and somehow it fails now to fall around her shoulders. A large wicker chest, enameled blue, sits in one corner and serves as her dresser. Walking now to it and lifting the lid, she begins to inspect the contents, to make her choices for the day. Without turning: "I need to dress. I am getting ready to go to the beach. Give me some privacy."

And so I do, but not quite; for as I pause momentarily outside her closed door, I hear the wicker lid drop shut and the sound of Zipper lying back on her bed. It is a sound I know as well as I know—now—that she will be staying at the house all day. It's not really clear to me why I know this; it simply makes me happy.

Now bristling with what should be exhilaration at facing another new day but is in fact psychosomatic alcohol withdrawal, I assess the hallway, find it in good order, and hasten to the big room for a gin and some morning television. It is rapidly approaching seven a.m., and I want to be sure to catch what I can of all three introductory indexes to each of the morning-network-magazine-news shows; barring any unusual complications, such as potentially interesting subject matter, I can then switch over to one of Los Angeles' myriad independents, who are never too proud to rerun a seventies sitcom or a titillating aerobics production at this or any other hour. Selecting a stool at the bar, I pour a generous glass of gin, condescendingly flash it at a suppliant bottle of tonic, and spin on my barstool. From here I can see the bank of TVs that sit on steel shelves that span the otherwise uselessly acute corner opposite the bar. I pick up one of the normally elusive but supposedly plentiful remotes that hide like mice about the room and turn on what turns out to be the upper right screen (they sit two over three). Unlike

Double Felix I am uncomfortable viewing more than one program at a given moment, though I am addicted to cycling back and forth through the channels, as long as I can keep track of what's on each one. Even viewing the same program on several screens—an option which seems to thrill the rest of the house—is for me disquieting, for I find I am unable to keep my eyes on any one screen; rather, they move about frantically, as if needing perpetual confirmation that the image displayed on each set is indeed identical to the others. I suppose I eschew the cable channels for similar reasons: they demand that too many options be addressed.

This bar—procured, incidentally, from an actual barroom in Double Felix's past, back when he might have been found in such a place and would have cared enough to take along a piece of it, way back before I knew him, before the whole reference came to be dismissed with a disparaging *Some place I was once in . . . closed down . . . took it off their hands*—is now serving as a line upon which I am a point. This is a geometrical approximation that amuses me, one that I tend to hide behind. Perhaps, though, the significance is lost when I'm sitting alone in the room, as I am now; and really, it is the wrong room for such a bar, for even during a party the drinkers who populate this bar are indulging speciously in the vice, never understanding the realities and terror of the habit, but always very impressed with their random stays in treatment programs and close calls that amount, at best, to just another Christmas tree light turned on behind their eyes. Unqualified attendees notwithstanding, I feel safer watching television from the bar. A child on the return trip, I can stay here in my specially designed womb and look at the evil world as it transpires before me, innocuous behind the convex glass of the picture tube.

As usual, the network morning shows fail to seduce me, and I find myself watching *The Love Boat*. A given episode of this show normally features three stories, three minicasts from a boatload of passengers who are all traveling together but for our purposes are visited alternately during the cruise. The segment that has my closest attention involves Captain Stubing, who is slated to be honored as this year's outstanding private citizen by The Rhinos, a group of adult male pranksters who are annoying everyone on board with their practical jokes but are tolerated because they reputedly do a lot of good charity and community work. Now, Captain Stubing is not a member of The Rhinos, but as captain, and out of deference to The Rhinos' good reputation, he reluctantly agrees to attend the impending awards ceremony and so, at the request of his benefactors, commences the impartial business of choosing which crew member will introduce him from the podium. Ultimately Isaac, the black bartender, is chosen through a random pin-the-tail-on-the-crew-member type improvisation in the crew's lounge, and if we didn't know any better, that would be that. But it seems that the head Rhino, upon hearing of Captain Stubing's selection, pulls him aside and, armed with a modicum of tact, makes it known that Isaac, while a great guy, is not exactly Rhino material. This is especially distressing to us because—even Captain Stubing doesn't know this—we know that innocent, happy-to-go-along, black Isaac didn't want to do it in the first place and was only following orders. Be that as it may, the quandary is in place, provided we accept that Captain Stubing's disposition regarding the award is analogous to his feelings about the incongruous charity-racism of the Rhinos; analogous, in fact, to whether he accepts racism along with charity, or rejects charity as well as racism. It would seem that these are his only two options.

But I blow it. Momentarily secure in the knowledge that all will be well, I turn to a local talk show and become transfixed by the cleavage of the guest, Cindi Trim, a local woman whose husband has financed what she claims is her lifelong dream, a bistro near Venice Beach called Graffiti. I gather that, in lieu of windows and in keeping with the spirit of the neighborhood as Cindi perceives it, she has installed large white panels on all exposed sides of the structure. She has even gone so far as to have cans of spray paint tethered to these panels with long elastic cords fastened at intervals of ten feet along the foundation. Magnanimously, Cindi vows that she will do whatever it takes to become a part of Venice; and indeed, I must confess that she looks every inch the good sport. But having absorbed her story, and with the faint howl of a panic calling from my gut, I realize that time has been sacrificed foolishly on this drivel, and that I actually did want to follow the progression of Captain Stubing's dilemma. Quickly, I grab the remote and switch back to *The Love Boat*, only to arrive too late—well, almost too late. The head Rhino, standing on the bridge and wearing that lesson-learned look, is sheepishly talking to Captain Stubing: He's sorry . . . he doesn't know where The Rhinos got off the track, but things are gonna change NOW . . . he wants to thank Captain Stubing and the whole crew, especially Isaac, for setting them straight. Clearly I have missed something important.

I marvel at Captain Stubing's abilities; the man is truly an epic hero. I want to ride *The Love Boat* to all its romantic ports of call, I want to do something nefarious—perhaps fuck a fifteen-year-old girl on its starboard deck—confident that I will be, nonetheless, digested by its facile morality. I want to know what I would have known if I had only stayed tuned. But I didn't. I missed the key part of this passage, and in a fit of frustration I throw the remote across the room, causing it to strike and permanently mar one of the murals. I don't care; how could I have so cockily changed the channel? How could I have missed this piece of magic? The television, in its desire to offer me everything, has fucked up and given me nothing. I will never know why The Rhinos are better men now, why Captain Stubing is the same man, and how this theoretically impossible creation of energy occurred. Or did something generate the spark? Was the energy given up? When was the click? Which nanosecond held the world in exactly the right position to make this come about? I can only deduce that Captain Stubing has in fact been imperceptibly altered, that, like all good saints, he gave up something of himself—with no regard for himself—simply because it had to be done. This may be a small thing, but because I lingered on chit-chatty cuisine served over a bed of cleavage, I have lost it—or failed to gain it. From where I sit I feel very undernourished, as if I just dotted the i on my American Express receipt and passed it back to a preoccupied Cindi Trim, her eight-fifty dinner salad a fleeting memory to my tongue, as well as to the saucer on which it came.

Thus I am found by Laurie, resplendent in a white terry cloth robe and matching crown.

"All cleaned up—freshly showered, are we?" I say.

Looking somehow official, she walks behind the bar without comment, as if to verify physically her position as taciturn barkeep. After inspecting the area and finally turning up a can of orange juice–like drink, she says, gauging my reaction, "I had a long, dirty night. Can I freshen your drink?"

"Yes." I don't want to hear anymore about her night. The idea of two other people making love is one that I often find conversationally disturbing. On top of that, in just the last few hours I have grown an inexplicable and probably unjustifiable dislike for Timmy.

"What can I pour for you so early this morning?" Seizing my half-empty glass, she spins a cocktail napkin into place. She looks comfortable behind the bar and is clearly enjoying herself.

"Just straight gin—you can add some of that orange stuff if you want—and I prefer to think of it as extremely late. You just missed *Love Boat*." I gesture with the back of my head to the TV, which now, judging from the earth-tone reflection dancing on my glass, is threatening to display either *Bonanza* or *The Big Valley* in consideration of the eight o'clock hour; shows for which I have no patience. "I guess we can safely turn it off now, though."

"No," she says, "that's okay. Let's leave it on." This actually comes as a bit of a relief since I'd rather not confess to throwing the remote across the room, something that might require explanation if I have to go looking for it. My drink arrives, freshened and sans orange stuff. Laurie leans forward on the bar, supported by her arms, elbows locked and hands spread wide: what's yer trouble, bub? "And did you and Double Felix have your little meeting this morning?"

"Yes. Always. Of course. You shoulda been there." Annoying— though probably originally euphonious—music buzzes forth from the television behind me. *Bonanza!* Galloping chords charge through the once still air of the room: *bum di di bum di di bum di di bum da da da, bum di di bum di di bum di di bum da da da da da daa*. I can feel the map of the Ponderosa ablaze on my back. Pixels combusting, spontaneously and aptly, open a portal to a world that for some reason could never earn the respect that I lavish on *The Love Boat*; perhaps I just find it easier to believe in a clean-shaven Gavin MacLeod than I do Dan Blocker: Hoss without a whisker. I say, "Mind if I at least change the channel?" (whoops)

"But then you would have to get up and find the little controller, right? Could be clean across the room by now." And leaning forward over the bar, very close to my face: "Tell me, William, do we even know if it's still operable?"

Fortunately my intoxication is now at such a level as to afford me only partial devastation. "So you have a habit of spying on hapless drunks. How very nice for you." I'm staring right at her, trying to outplay her, but I suspect my intoxication is likewise at a level that has rendered such a calculated maneuver prohibitively difficult. I further suspect that girls like Laurie are outmaneuvered only in James Bond movies, that in this real world they are always at the helm of any situation they place themselves in.

She narrows her eyes, tilts her head, raises her nose, and says, "Did you mention to Mr. D. Felix that I would like a word with him—or I guess I should say that I would like him to have a word with me? Did you, William, as would have been pursuant to your promise? Should I expect a summons this morning? This afternoon?"

This has me feeling about ten years old. I obviously can't describe my conversation with Double Felix this morning, much less her place in it; rather, I mumble, "Well, something went wrong. We didn't really get around to it. I mean, actually, Double Felix suggested that I speak to you, that I ask you to fill me in on the world at large. I don't get out much." (unfortunate)

"So my name did come up then?"

"Um . . . yeah, I guess. But really more as an incidental device to insult me than as a preface to a discussion of you." (unlikely)

The skillful woman first, she decides to go with, "Insult you? Why would he want to insult you? You're such a nice guy, why would anyone want to insult you?" Removing the towel from her head, she swings her hair back and around. Disheveled, it falls mostly on and in front of her left shoulder. She tugs at her robe as if this is an indicated adjustment. I am given cleavage; she knows she looks good. "Do you still want to watch something else? Shall I find the little controller for you?"

I have the distinct impression that no response is required from me to any of this; in fact, I'm sure that no response is desired. By way of a sign of life, I vaguely shake my head: naw.

And like I'm watching some sort of wet dream/nightmare, she pulls the end of the cloth belt around her waist, causing her robe to fall open. Though her breasts remain covered and her pussy (panties?) is blocked from my view by her proximity to the bar, the vision is still breathtaking, and I predictably turn to Jell-O.

"Nothing?" she says. "He didn't even mention whether or not he wants to sleep with me? Or you, William, you didn't talk about me at all? You didn't even speculate, in that noble male fashion, about how I would be in bed? Aren't you the least bit interested in me? Do I look that bad?" She takes a meaningful step backward now, touches her own hips in a manner that suggests she is using the arms of a stranger. (no panties)

One glimpse, and I avert my eyes. I can't look; it's too much right now; it goes beyond fun, sex, or desire; it's truly uncomfortable.

"Fine. You look fine," I say with what I hope is a not-too-audible quiver in my voice. "But I'm sorry, Double Felix and I didn't talk about you this morning. I thought about you, though." I'm still looking at the wall, I suppose trying to look pensive. "Would you hand me that gin bottle, please, Laurie?"

She regards me silently for a moment, her lips pursed, her robe still open. "Oh, I'm sure you can reach it yourself, William," she says.

As she strides out of the room her robe flows and sweeps the air, still open, more in mocking antagonism now, less in teasing. I turn to the TV for solace but instead am given participation in a test of the Emergency Broadcast System. I wasn't aware they still did these things; they seem a memory restricted to my childhood. In any case, my watch indicates that I am pushing twenty minutes into *Bonanza*, and I again consider retrieving the remote.

Not the total schoolboy, I know that there was no more chance of me making love to Laurie a moment ago than there had been years earlier with any of the many salacious strippers I used to leer at, when I really was a schoolboy and enamored with such women. But such as I am, openly human, albeit not as lucid as I ought to be, I regret my failure, regret that it compelled her to market her goods penultimately in an act that was in some ways tantamount to prostitution. Laurie, despite her intrepidity, is likely not made of such fiber—as is, say, Zipper or myself—though I doubt she knows it, and could react badly. I feel I have wronged her, and in this she has unwittingly furthered her seduction of me. There are things . . . things about her I admire, things I guess I want to somehow emulate, but what they are I don't know. She is oddly familiar, like a lost cousin or the daughter of a close friend. I am totally infatuated with this girl.

Rising, I shuffle over to the mural I damaged earlier. I was wrong; the damage is not permanent; rather, it is apparently only a small black line drawn by the plastic trim of the remote: a high-velocity crayon. It will be wiped off by whoever attends to such things. Ironically, it forms a little arrow, and following its directive, my eyes are led to the remote, under a sofa and barely visible. I retrieve it and drop onto the sofa. As I click the power off button, a gunshot on *Bonanza* is replaced with a loud but probably harmless crash from Double Felix's bedroom, which is behind one of the walls that hold the television rack—sitting, in effect, on the other side of the blank screens I am now facing.

As with Zipper and Laurie, I managed to somehow fail Double Felix this morning. Looking at my reflection in the dormant TV screens, I can pretty much imagine him there in his room, perhaps wincing, clutching at a newly bruised shin, laughing at a newly broken object, briefly mourning some recently spilt vodka. I move back to the bar and my gin, carrying the remote, my prize, though I choose not to use it now; instead, I keep my eye on the screens—this time all of them simultaneously. They are my window to Double Felix as he is at this moment, at eight and three-fifths o'clock this morning.

Alone in his room sits he. The door is closed—perhaps locked—and it is this that he hates and likes the best. His mind, always preoccupied, is dwelling deeply on something, on one thing. There is a tremor in his hand when he holds it in a certain position, and this is odd, for his experience tells him that such anomalies are strictly limited to the first minutes of the morning and should have been drank well away by now. The door to the balcony stands away from its jamb a few inviting inches, but stands nonetheless ignored; the day outside has blossomed far too well to abide his participation, he thinks. Conversely, his room is nested in The Place Created By Him, and so he chooses now to stay in it, feels it's an okay place for him to be. He had been rummaging through his desk (possibly the wrong word—items were lifted and replaced carefully, methodically—such is his manner) but then stopped abruptly. It was on the return to his chair that he walked into the small table, knocking it over, barking his shin, and causing the crash that I heard. He may be distracted, as am I, by Laurie. She is bewitching, and I, at least, am smitten. His eyes wander, pause on a heretofore unobserved crack in the plaster of his ceiling, then another, and he muses on the propagational nature of such things. He is seated for over a full minute before he realizes his drink was on the table and hence is now on the floor. Rising to get another, he becomes disoriented and can't remember where one would go in his room to fetch a glass of vodka. But then . . . yes, he walks to the bar and prepares his drink: a happy ending, but only after a disturbing new twist that will not be ignored. Oh, I would say he is acting more like me than ever before; yes, I would take that ground, I would venture that. Like a child (dare I say), he digs Laurie and is temporarily overwhelmed. Well, welcome to the club! See there, in the top left screen, how he sweats, again in his chair. He thinks there is a cockroach in his room, jerks around to look, but it is nothing—maybe a flaw in his cornea. Eyes forward. More sweat.

"Just look at this studio . . ."

Awakening now. Short nap—still on the couch, but noise from all the televisions.

". . . filled with glamorous merchandise . . ."

Yes, someone has turned on all of the TVs. I was staring at them earlier; they were off then. Evidently I fell asleep for—just after ten, still morning—a short while, and someone came in and turned on the TVs.

". . . fabulous and exciting bonus prizes . . ."

My drink seems to be missing too, though it appears that I'm the only one here right now. Sitting up, I gather myself for a trip to the bar and a fresh drink.

". . . including . . ."

This is one of those crossroad times of the day. A few months ago I might have used this opportunity to have a cup of coffee and some eggs and more or less sober up for the bulk of the afternoon. Granted, it was always a debate, but lately I don't even bother thinking it over; coffee and eggs just aren't appropriate anymore. I get up and make my way over to the bar where I happily find remotes for all the televisions in a neat row and mute the lot of them. More like some sort of insect's-eye dream now, Vanna silently waltzes with and around her merchandise in wonderful quint-o-vision. Suitably impressed, I secretly want to provide the ooohs and ahhs that I know are emanating from the videotape in Burbank only to be blocked by my reckless button pushing. I prepare my drink as a more modest version than earlier—this one contains actual tonic—so I won't be so likely to drop off again, for I already feel far too adequately rested. I think I feel far too adequate in general, unless I'm confusing what I am with what I aspire to be. With my pacemaking gin et al. in hand, and the five televisions, apparently unaware of my de facto forfeiture of any consumer status that I may have once enjoyed, desperately and silently screaming at my back in one final plea for my attention, I cruise out of the big room and toward the French doors across the hall and the deck to which they lead.

They lead to my best shot, these French doors. Passing through them, I squint that self-satisfied squint of one who knows he is legitimately exploiting a theatrical visage: Walk into sun. Squint. Chin up. Know everything. Handle anything—a stiff neck, a hangover, being out of ice—anything. This is my turf, the deck. Once a subset of Double Felix's turf, I now think of it in another way: Double Felix's house is a superset of my turf. This is my big attempt at self-confidence, my self-study assertiveness training. Trying to view things in such a manner, I hope, will give me a more direct connection to the world at large, and indeed, standing out here on my deck, I feel almost six feet tall—just two inches shy of my actual height.

Though the deck faces west, the house is set in such a way that the summer provides direct sunlight by this time in the morning, and Zipper, looking uncharacteristically monochrome in her white bikini, is sunning in my favorite chaise. Light on dark: she is a South American art object that is inexplicably being refired in a California kiln; perhaps this piece is a little too hard to understand, yet doesn't have the decency to remain relegated to the lower level, behind the glass and across from the Egyptian room.

"Waiting for your date to wake up and get wired for the beach?" I say, but not without some appreciative affection. We both know she's not going anywhere today.

"I guess my date is here. Did you have a nice nap? Are you going to be not so cranky now?" She deferentially makes to rise and surrender my chaise.

"No, no stay—please," I say, sitting down on the end of a nearby but as yet un-thoroughly-tested-for-reclining-much-less-sleeping chaise. "I plan to take a big walk along the railing in just a couple of minutes. You can sit here and supervise in case I get lost."

"Yes, I can see how you might get lost inside this railing. Especially you." She looks over at the French doors to make sure they're closed and that we're alone outside the house. "I'm glad you came out here. I want to talk to you." And indeed she does appear to have reached some sort of conclusion, though the unfamiliar hint of rehearsal in her words makes me doubt that I'll be privy to it.

I've always admired Zipper's sparing use of language; in fact, I see it as a reflection of her clear thinking. She has the words she uses and uses the words she has. This is an improvement over my own tangled attempts at communication, which are often tedious and prolix to a fault, due chiefly to a pedantic father who once gave me a list of the two hundred most widely used words in the English language and, shocked by my difficulty in augmenting that list, demanded that I add ten words each week, using all of them in a conversation, the effectiveness of which had a direct bearing on the timely disbursement of my allowance. Even my thoughts, as nearly as I can tell, are convoluted beyond useful-ness by my silent, internal quest for the precise words and phrasing. I invariably end up very unsure of the basis of my original reasoning, the fiber of what I wanted to reflect and store in the murk of my gray matter. But Zipper, with her implied subjects and monosyllabic nouns, her intransitive verbs and three-letter adjectives, rarely fails to make herself well understood, and I can only wonder at the clarity of vision she must enjoy when communicating with herself; though here I may be far from the mark: a person such as she might not share my penchant for self-conversation, mental masturbation, or secretly smug schizophrenia, annotated with a Cross pen and time-stamped pursuant to the positioning of a Rolex's pretty little hands.

"Oh? Do You Want To Talk To Me?" I say, gently teasing her by mocking, with only symbolic success, her less-than-fluid diction. Then, seeing that I have successfully conjured up the familiar, condescendingly patient smile that she saves for such remarks: Are you having fun? Are you satisfied? I am satisfied and decide to signal that I am ready to move into new territory. "That's a pretty bikini. Is it new? You wear it well. Isn't it . . . um . . . sort of white? I mean it looks great on you, but you tend to wear more colorful . . . stuff." And because I can't resist: "Or did you just misunderstand the Clorox commercial?" Maybe I'm not ready to move into new territory.

She looks down at her bikini, regarding it as if indeed there was some sort of laundry blunder that has heretofore gone unnoticed. "No. It is white, that's all. It is plain white. It is new, but I don't like it too much. I sent my other ones out and this was all I could find to wear. I don't think it is a very good color on me, but you have to let me talk to you anyway, okay?"

"Okay," I say, laughing, amused at her innocently contrived compound. My normally adroit little Zipper loses the color from her bathing suit and with it suddenly goes her ability to think in linear terms: a

bleached bucket non sequitur. A victim of an abused coordinating con-
junction, herself a temporarily censored colorful metaphor. But I can
see she is oddly uncomfortable with my scrutiny of her suit, and I always
care about what she has to say. I lean back in the chaise, keep my hand
on my drink, and feel the ice melt somewhere near the logical center of
whatever cylinder may be defined by the wrap of my hand, diluting it
further, silently deferring to Zipper's silent requests. I know her; she will
never wear this bikini again. "I want you to talk to me."

The sun is full on her, its light bouncing off her before being sucked
in by my eyes; that is, more of it has gone askew than I can manage to
suck in right now, less than I would normally like to suck—perhaps never
enough. She is happening an infinitesimal moment before I know about
it. I wonder if this can be fixed, for now we are merely contemporaneous.
How is it that I feel simultaneous with Laurie? She is a stranger. I wonder
why I'm in love with Laurie, why I'm sure I would willingly castrate myself
at her request, provided she would watch. I take a deep breath and detect
a disagreeable . . . something. There is an odor in the house, a faint odor
that is unique to this house. I began to notice it after being here for a
year or so, though anytime I have mentioned it I've been met with blank
stares. Very subtle, I can't describe it. It was not so bad at first, gone with
any open window, but I've grown to dislike it. Now I smell it out here,
on the deck, for the first time—just a touch, probably my imagination. I
must be getting sober, so with no little effort, I stand and walk to the bar.
Zipper's eyes follow me, though she seems distracted. I fill my glass.

"Well . . . why are you drinking too much?" she blurts out. She
winces—actually winces—as these words cross her lips, and for the first
time since I have known Zipper, I get a strong sensation that she is doing something distasteful to her; indeed, this is not a question that I
expected to hear from her.

I look up from my drink quizzically, though really I'm just plain shocked and am trying to piece together a response. "Do . . . um. Is . . . Are you . . ." More gin, perhaps, yes. I give up and say, "Have we just met?" Even this slight levity, however, is evidently not appropriate; this I gather from her gravely determined countenance. I gather further that there is no escape, and frankly, I don't want one. Zipper is a person from whom I am willing to listen to this kind of rubbish—if only to find out from whence it sprung—so I go directly back to my seat and take it.

"Don't make a joke, you heard me," she says. She looks angry, but I know her well and can see that in truth she is feeling uncomfortable, acting almost sheepish behind her words. "You're always drunk! Look how this morning you fell asleep. You passed out so early this morning." She leans forward. "I watched you sleep. You kept making noise, you almost screamed once. You never used to make noise when you slept," she says, and in the echo I hear: with me.

"So I'm dreaming—so what? What are you saying? This isn't like you."

"Well it's like me now." With this, a look away, out over the water, then: "You should go to one of those hospitals on television, one up in the mountains . . . then you should get a job and move away from here." Still watching the ocean, she snaps her lips shut as if to try to catch the tail end of her sentence and suck it back in before it reaches my ears.

I am flabbergasted—something I hoped never to be. Like a misleading movie trailer, recut for a desperate promotion and now proudly flaunting fists and ass in hyperactive cutaways, Zipper's words must have very little to do with her actual concern, and this is the tack I take.

I fix my face in such a way as to indicate that I am taking this seriously—which I am—and ask her, "What are you really saying to me?" though I know I won't find out, at least not now.

And Zipper, enigmatic, true to her hemisphere, true to my expectations, says merely, "I am just worried about you," and with this, it would seem, the verbal part of today's topic is closed.

So, as I seem to be lost in unfamiliar waters anyway, I plunge further and lean back on the still untested chaise, though for an instant my eyes do drift longingly to my usual lounge, still under Zipper. I keep my muscles tense, as if this will somehow save me should things fail and abandon me to the oak with a crash. Eventually, though, this strange new bed gains my confidence; perhaps it can serve as my temporary backup, to be used reluctantly on occasions such as this. Unbuttoning my shirt, I close my eyes and concentrate on the reassuringly functional sensation of sweat issuing from my pores. The sun has gained a fine purchase in the sky, and it is from there that it works so indifferently on me.

We are both silent for a long time, then Zipper says, "Laurie."

"What?" I say too quickly, worried that Laurie has joined us without my knowledge. I look around; we are still alone.

"I am thinking," she continues, "you should spend some time with Laurie, before she gets bored and leaves. It would be good for you to have some new influence."

We turn to each other. Not sure of what this all means, I remain silent, though I again wonder what Zipper knows of Timmy and Laurie.

"Don't worry about Timmy," she says. "She is not interested in him. She is only looking for something to do." Then at the ocean: "I think she is looking for you."

"I think you'd better find one of your old bikinis pretty quick," I say. "This one is metamorphosing you through its insidious whiteness." Of course, I feel that I should thus dutifully dismiss her suggestion.

But she flares: "This is not a joke. I am serious and you are talking like a schoolboy." Then more evenly: "Do not worry about me. I'll still be your little toy if things go bad." And finally, with affection: "I only want you to be happy. I think this is what you should do."

"Well, my love," I say, "you are most certainly thinking something." I drain my drink for punctuation and an ice cube falls from the bottom of the upturned glass and hits me in the nose.

She frowns. "You need this. Just listen to me. You always say how smart I am, so just listen to me . . ."

"You know," I say, interrupting—something I rarely do—"what makes you think it's that easy? I mean Laurie is not exactly enamored of me." This is of course a mistake, this open acknowledgment of the possibility, and though all my experience tells me I'm fucking up, the fact is that I'm already too caught up in it, too intrigued by the remote chance that Zipper has some hitherto undisclosed magic with which she could make such a thing happen. I am reminded of a middle-aged gym teacher whose calisthenic and occasionally moral tutelage I was once under—no doubt during the hapless blur that was sixth to eighth grades. If he were with me now, perhaps in the form of a bald and sweaty little angel on my shoulder, he would advise me not to let the little head do my thinking for me. But he is not here, and so remains consistent in his uselessness to me.

What is it about Laurie that I've missed? First with Double Felix over Morning Vodka and now with Zipper, the mere mention of the name tends to send conversation in the strangest directions, making me glad to be drunk and so have a place to hide. What I'm not really considering is the deeper aspect of all this; that is, maybe Zipper's right. Maybe I really do need Laurie. It is a truly fantastic notion, and I'm not sure what the ultimate implications are. Presumably a relationship with Laurie would be the beginning of the end of my protracted stay here at the house, for she is clearly not the sort of girl to stick around and rot in this sunny little hole. So . . . what? A job? Marriage? An apartment? A house? Lunches, flat tires, buses, being early, being late, shopping, tow-away zones? These are all things to which I can no longer assign meaning. And yet, somehow, the appeal of a real life, of all those things, is ineffably strong and rooted more deeply in myself than I care to look.

Zipper. Could it be that she is this good, that she is this selfless? I am inclined to wonder what her motive is, but she is not a person who works in motives, or at least not in the impurity that has come to be connected with that word. I could bring myself to tears if I worked too long on this, for it is possible that Zipper has given up on her own ability to save me—assuming that I require saving—and is therefore searching for another course of action, a Plan B. Or maybe she just wants me out of her hair. Either way, it would seem that at least one of us is not doing their job.

"Oh!" she groans in frustration. "You are so stupid! How would you know what she likes? Have you even tried? I do not think so. I think you have played little games with her and told yourself that you have tried. I do not think you have tried to make love to her any more than you have tried to do anything lately."

This, of course, is yet another can of very unappetizing worms, one that I'd rather not look into right now. Instead I say, "But didn't you tell me just a few hours ago that you think she's destructive? Remember that? You said destructive. You said she was *destructive.*" Yousaiddestructive yousaiddestructive nanananananaaa. What a brat I am, eyeyamm!

I think the last time I expressed myself so eloquently was in a dispute over the last remaining Jell-O cube in my elementary school cafeteria. I need some more gin but don't want to go and pour it; I feel it would alter the course of an already circuitous conversation. I sniff at my glass instead.

Pressed lips, then simply: "I was wrong. She is very pretty, and I was just jealous. Now I have had time to think, and for you she is a good thing . . . for us. I mean that it is a good thing that she is here. It is time we all thought about some changes—especially you." She rises from her lounge and, reaching for my glass, says, "I will get you more gin. Then I'm going for a little walk. I want to stretch my legs."

Still on the deck with me, I feel her, and still again after she leaves, though here I am cogently alone. A misty Zipper mystery is everywhere around me as it predictably fills the vacuum left by her words. It seems to me that we are never so alone as we are when another who is close to us affects distance. Nowhere in my Zipper guidebook do I see a reference to behavior such as this. Why does she want me to be with Laurie? If I leave my own libido behind for a moment, I find I must ask myself: what could anyone possibly gain from such an implausible relationship?

It's almost eleven o'clock, and for lack of a better diversion, I decide to take a shower. But I am interrupted on the short trip to my room by the shrill sound of Maggie's less than euphonious voice. In the big room, positioned behind a large wire-frame sculpture, she is not at all unlike some oversized obnoxious parrot squawking for a WormNip—or whatever it is that parrots eat.

"William! Will-fucking-yam!" She is truly a goddess. Apparently she does not see me, and though it might be entertaining to remain silent and let her continue, there are others present.

"Right here, Maggie," I say, stepping into the big room. I see now that she is standing next to a stocky young man dressed in green with the legend *Here-N-Gone Xpress* sewn in greener onto his cap of greenest. "Good morning, Maggie." I cross the room to where they stand at the front door.

"Fuck you too, William," she says. "This pain-in-the-ass says he has something for you, and he won't give it to anyone else." She folds her arms in exasperation and, as if to underscore all the trouble I'm causing, rolls her eyes.

The messenger, either too easily convinced that I am who I'm purported to be, or understandably anxious to make his delivery and leave, says to me, "I have something for you, sir. If you'll just sign here . . ." and he offers me a clipboard.

Signing, I accept the small envelope from his hand. I am about to thank him when I realize I have no money in my pockets with which to tip him. A quick look around the room for succor reveals only Maggie, returned now to the couch, Timmy, and Laurie. All of them watching all of the televisions and sipping coffee. No help there, so I grab a new fifth of Wild Turkey from behind the bar and hand it to him. He looks at the bottle, hesitates (probably worried that I may be a corporate officer of Here-N-Gone and that this is a test), then takes it and leaves. I move to the bar, where I sit and open the envelope.

"Whadya get, Bill?" says Timmy, still staring at the TVs, but canting his head as if he is on the verge of looking at me. I have seen him remain like this for fifteen or twenty minutes at a time.

Not bothering to look up or speak, I lift a finger: just a minute while I open it. Though I'm sure he misses my gesture, he keeps quiet. Communicating with this group makes me feel ridiculous—I find Timmy particularly annoying this morning—but not responding would make me feel even more ridiculous.

No one is concerned as I spend an inordinate amount of time examining the single sheet of paper that alone was contained in the envelope. It takes me three readings before the bizarre missive even begins to make sense:

William,

    This message is extremely confidential. Tell of or show it to no one.

    Please visit me in my room.

D.F.

(dictated but not read)

Of course I immediately think that it is a note from Double Felix asking me to go to his room, but then I remember the messenger and try again. D.F. . . . D.F. . . . Who is D.F.? What could it mean, visit me in my room? I look again around the room—as if they would be any more help to me now than they were a moment ago. Soon enough, though, I see that it is a note from Double Felix. What else could it be? Moreover, why should I be surprised? The man is nothing if not creative.

"Well? Aren't you going to share it with us? I mean, I did have to get up and answer the fucking door." This from Maggie, who is sitting next to Laurie, the latter typically quiet and observant.

"Sorry, Maggie," I say, folding the evidence into my pocket and, for some childish reason, gloating.

But she is not satisfied with this. Assuming the role of house-crier, she announces, "Good news, everybody! Zipper's work permit just arrived. Now she can start fucking William again and get them both off of everyone's nerves!"

Though uncalled for, this remark is, I must confess, unusually quick for Maggie; I am impressed despite myself. I recall when I first saw her. Like Double Felix, I was . . . well, aroused—she is very striking. She is also young, and this only adds to her nubility. She won't give it up, but

Double Felix and I place her in her mid-twenties. I remember how she unwittingly reassured me of my own maturity and levelheadedness as I, demonstrating uncharacteristic bighead thinking in fortuitous deference to my aforementioned erstwhile gym teacher, put my natural prurience on hold as I came to understand just what an indefatigable bitch she really is. For now I, untroubled and thus superior, am content simply to wink at her as I stroll from the big room and toward Double Felix's room. There I will find, carefully palmed by the puzzle maker, the key piece to this strange little puzzle.

Locked and initially unresponsive, his door requires three sets of knocks and a ridiculous *or else* (proceeded by *It's William, open this door*) before it finally yields to my desquirmination and swings open, a studied Double Felix at the knobby control.

"William. Please hustle on in here, my friend, so that we might have some privacy. You are in receipt of my message, I gather." Moving around me in a half-circle, he ushers me past the door, which he promptly locks behind us. "So we did connect after all," he says, now standing at his bar. "Your lunch proposal, albeit somewhat early. I believe it's gin for you at this advanced hour."

I pluck the drink from his hand, and as one we sit in the two low and rather retentive overstuffed chairs that serve as monstrous guardians of the petite table between them.

"Not exactly the most efficient way to get ahold of me," I say, waving the paper through the air before setting it down on the table.

He grins. "Yes, it was a long way to go, but I could think of no better way to get you in here without anyone knowing that I had asked you." He shrugs his shoulders as if this is both obvious and conclusive.

"But why don't you want anyone to know that you asked me to your room?" I say, and detecting in my voice a tinge of frustration, I add, "Are we finally going to fuck or something?"

Matter-of-factly: "Because they would wonder why I didn't just come out and get you."

I snort and rub my eye—one of those gestures that we all learn through mimicry. I feel as though I've been driving for hours only to arrive at my point of origin. "Well why didn't you just come out and get me?"

"Oh," he says, blinking. "I suppose that's a good question. I'm sorry, William. It's just that I've been preoccupied with Laurie. See, that's the problem. I can't risk running into Laurie, at least not right now. I'm just not ready. I had to talk to you first." He stops, starts, then stops again. Finally: "I just couldn't go out there . . . I couldn't."

An empty beat.

I am moved by his sincerity and . . . regular-guyness; he seems so basic all of a sudden: a teenager confessing to his pal that he is lovesick. The day continues to be full of surprises as I am shown this new side of the polygon that is Double Felix. The guy needs to talk with me: What a wonderful feeling! I feel closer to him at this moment than I would if we were finally fucking.

"William," he says, a look of crazed determination in his eyes, "I am in love with Laurie." Then as an afterthought: "Oh, I realize that I hardly know her."

Being none too swift of thought lately, it is just now dawning on me that there may be some potential conflict here. Even if my own preferences are set aside for the moment, it would seem that what Zipper wants—or thinks she wants—is now at odds with what Double Felix wants. How typical that the two people closest to me—practically the only two people I know—have fortuitously managed to step on each other's toes in the same eventful morning of an otherwise uneventful year.

Double Felix leaps from his chair—actually, he tries to but ends up climbing out of it—and begins to dance around me enthusiastically as if to help dissipate the energy that mere talking won't release. "Now, William, I know we said all sorts of things this morning—we always do—but I've been working this over. Over, over, over." This repeated while spinning around. "Foremost in this matter, it is your guidance I seek. But you can see that I am already more or less decided . . ." He stops briefly; in fact his delivery is heavily punctuated with physical stops, jerks, and false starts. ". . . probably more from where you're sitting. Now, again, as you know, I have only just made her acquaintance, as it were, but I am nonetheless refreshingly decided—regarding this matter, that is. And most clear indeed—shall I say perspicuous?—about what I plan to do, which is . . . Say! Was it my imagination, or did a shadow cross your face this morning—what was the word? Yes: chicaning. That was it! I used the word chicaning, and you looked slightly—well, frankly, obtuse. But only for the slimmest of seconds, William, and yes, of course, most uncharacteristically so, most uncharacteristically so. So here it is! We can better ourselves. We can learn. Lookitup, William, for witness me, mired in relative nescience only a few short hours ago. No more! Now I stand at the rock of resolution, brandishing my Excalibur, arm in arm with my good and true brother, William. Yea, were it that you were my brother of the blood, I could love you no more well than I do at this moment. And, of-fucking-course, all the other moments, the fine and not-so-fine lineage of moments that has delivered us to this one, the first, last, ineffable moment. Oh, I see that you see that I . . . am being rather effusive." He stops directly before me, dropping his voice and shoulders. "Many years ago, in another, much more abject room than this, I got very drunk for the sole purpose of hiding my last one hundred–dollar bill. I intentionally waited until I thought I was in what would become a blackout—quantity and experience my clues—and then hid the damn thing, thus in effect hiding it from my sober self and precluding its reckless or otherwise impulsive expenditure. Unfortunately, I managed also to preclude the eventual expenditure of the rent and was forced from the room, for I never was able to find the bill." He chuckles at this. I do too. Double Felix falls to his knees and says, "What am I thinking, William? I don't believe I know."

I think of Zipper; how would the great distiller of English respond? "You love Laurie," I say.

"Right." He nods introspectively, as if I am truly recalling this to him. "Right, and so you can understand why I have to ask you to direct your attentions elsewhere." Patting my knee, he stands and returns to his chair, drops into it like a dead fish on a deck.

Given that experience has proved to be no guide for coping with Double Felix today, this little bombshell is that much easier to absorb. "Are you serious?" I say. "Isn't this sort of new territory for you?"

Looking a tad wounded, he says, "We're not fraternity boys here, William. I did muddle through a few years without the benefit of your company. I'm sure you'll agree that a forty-one-year-old man ought to be capable of adult love, devotion, monogamy, and all that other stuff." A grin—not too wounded.

"Are you saying . . . what, you're gonna ask her to marry you?" Admittedly, this is sort of a nonquestion, but I'm still trying to figure out what my reaction to this is.

"I plan to spend some time with her first, but I wouldn't rule that out as an eventuality."

We say nothing for a time, him waiting for me to speak, me waiting for something to say. Finally I toss out, "Excuse me for being so quiet, it's just that I'm a bit surprised. Um . . . well, I wasn't aware that you two had spent any time together." In fact, working it over in my head, I can't recall seeing them even talking once at that party three days ago. Double Felix disappeared into his room right after finding her on the sofa the next morning and telling her to help herself to an empty room. Now that I think about it, even this traditional ceremony was muttered and terse, not so much as a nod given to the usual protracted orientation for which he has a penchant.

"You're right. We haven't actually been introduced—not formally, anyway."

Now I'm wondering if he knows about Timmy and his bride-to-be. "I should probably tell you that she spent the night down the hill with Timmy. At least, I'm pretty sure she did. She seems sort of—you know—friendly." How odd this feels, dancing around Double Felix with carefully chosen words about a woman!

He may have winced; I don't know. Caught off guard as I am, it's doubtful that I am being the accurate reporter that I normally endeavor to be.

"Matters such as this will in time be worked out between she and me," he says. "After all, she is merely a young girl who has yet to be acclimated to the lofty ideals I will present to her in due course."

I wait for the smile, but it doesn't come. Apparently this is not sarcasm. "You may rely on me," I say with a brave smile, though I wonder if he may.

I move to stand, but the damn chair, always impossible to rise from, regains me facilely with the help of my alcohol-managed equilibrium. Heavily involved in my struggle, I nonetheless notice that Double Felix is similarly trapped. We must appear quite comical, hopping on our asses and otherwise futilely writhing in the grip of these voluminous chairs, but neither one of us laughs.

CHAPTER FIVE

Only Maggie, alone and looking somewhat bewildered, remains in the big room as I wander in. Recently she has been treating us to her day look. This is the premakeup look that allows her to experience the morning—she used to hole up in her room till well after lunch. But lest anyone misunderstands and thinks that the a.m. face she wears is really her face, Maggie underscores her inchoate morning side with blatant down-dressing. Since the last thing that Maggie does is understate, these morning outfits can be quite wretched, to say the least. Most often she clings to a gray sweat suit that seems to grow grayer on a daily basis, but this morning she has truly undone herself. Her red hair is concealed under a green Day-Glo bandanna; her pants look to be half of a man's blue and light blue checked suit; over her vital signs she is wearing some sort of soiled brown bra which looks like it was ordered out of a 1956 sickroom supplies catalog. There are stains resembling blood on the bandanna, an actual smudge on her cheek. I think that Maggie thinks she is dressing the role of a supersardonic housewife, and I find myself suddenly enchanted by her and the harmless sparring she can so willingly provide.

Wordlessly I plop down next to her on the couch, almost too close. She grunts, and we watch TVs awhile, though I don't recognize the program, a videotaped sitcom.

"Get your pressing matter taken care of?" she finally says, but in a voice more monotone and less sarcastic than the words themselves.

"Yep. Thanks," I respond, and she looks at me for the first time. "Drink?" I ask as I rise to make one for myself.

"Uh uh. Not everyone's a fucking drunk, Willie."

"You're right. I'm sorry," I say, sitting right back down. My body is telling me it's time for a drink, and if I don't answer soon there will be hell to pay. This will all fit in nicely here; I'm in the mood for some pain, a hurdle or two.

She eyes me suspiciously. Abstinence, even the very thought of it, makes me horny.

Pivoting in her direction, I swing my arm over and behind her head and say, "Hey Maggie, wanna fuck?" I think I'm serious, and I have no idea why.

"What's the game? Huh? Trouble with your Zipper? Maybe Double Felix still won't sleep with you—is that it? How do you earn your keep around here, William? At least I hit the turf for him. What do you do, other than make heavy talk with your little whore?"

This is okay. How else could she possibly react to what I said? "I don't know, Maggie. Maybe I'm on deck. Maybe he's keeping me ready as Plan B. Let's face it, baby . . ." I almost remind her that she won't last forever, but decide to avoid that particular little cruelty. ". . . I can give him things that you can't."

"It's noon," she says. "Would you rather watch *The Brady Bunch* or *Hogan's Heroes?*"

"And I can give you things that he can't," I say, now stroking her hair.

She's beginning to suspect that I'm for real, and the thought is worrying at her feminine side, gnawing, perhaps, at the elastic of her panties. This would be where she lives her meticulously reckless life, for she is a careful girl.

"What?" she says. "What can you give me that he can't? You can't even tell me whether we should watch *The Brady Bunch* or *Hogan's Heroes.*" One by one she picks up the remotes from the table and turns off all the televisions. Giving me an inch, she relaxes her neck and feeds the back of her head to my hand: an itch to scratch.

I win, and so I squeeze her neck, pull her hair gently, then not so gently. "Let's go to your room," I say.

"Why?" she says. "Are you afraid Zipper will walk in on us?"

"Yes," I tell her, because that is what she wants to hear; because it may well be her angle, and I don't want to blow it now (because it's true).

I am trembling and in need of a drink. Mostly due to my anticipative imagination—for it hasn't been that long—it nonetheless hurts, and I like it. We go to her room. She actually leads me by the hand.

This girl has red hair. She would like to show me what she considers her bad side, but I have put myself in a position that makes this difficult for her. I find myself unexpectedly unconcerned with what she is; rather, I want proof now that she is.

I haven't been inside of Maggie's room since she took it over, and the teenage-esqe clutter notwithstanding, neither, would I say, has Maggie. Despite the fact that she has lived in this room for six months and intends to stay much longer, the place looks pretty much like a motel room that has been occupied only for the night. Substantially similar, this room remains, to the room that she spent her first night here in. Nothing new on the walls, furniture all in its generic position, it looks simply like an empty room after a dirty-laundry-and-beauty-product storm.

She pushes me on the bed; something with Velcro on it nestles in the small of my back. Maggie stands tall above me and removes her clothing. "I haven't showered yet this morning, so I may be a little ripe," she says, kneeling to me, playing for me a rhythm that is so bitter, so medicinal.

Back at the bar in the big room it is not yet one o'clock—a tribute to Maggie's efficiency—and I am happily looking down at a tall glass of cold gin. I left her, my antithetic angel, to go about her business: the killing of time, I presume, and whatever else may jump in her path. Our parting was predictably uncomfortable, plagued with embarrassment and stung with acrimony; I cannot forgive her for the former, can never repay her for the latter. To the surprise of no one, my service was badly performed; then, to the extreme surprise of William, Maggie was unpleasantly surprised.

So here I sit, alone in this big big room. A rubber ball metronomically pounds the outside wall, returning surely to Timmy's available hand; he is given to dancing around the driveway while mastering the dynamics of spheres. Double Felix remains sequestered in his room thinking of Laurie, who might be anywhere for all I know. Maggie is in her shower, probably masturbating, and Zipper is . . . where?

Ice cubes, spurious and thus doubly-negative tea leaves floating in my glass, impart to me a clairvoyance, one that is for my purposes (as I should be for Zipper's purposes, so shall she serve now for my purposes—she and Maggie). In my glass: both. In the shower: one. Standing undetected outside the shower: the other, less than one hundred feet and sixty-some seconds from where I now stand.

"I don't think that kind of dirt will wash off," says Zipper, startling Maggie with her presence. Middle finger extended in an unpracticed gesture, she draws in the condensation on the outside of the shower stall door the letter Z, but she is only vaguely aware of the literary allusion, originating less than one hundred miles and sixty-some years from where she now stands.

Not given to the European penchant for self-control, it was all she could do to not accost me as I strode from my wayward fuck nest. My chiding can wait; the berating of Maggie can't. Hell, I'm probably not even all that guilty in her adoring eyes (this sounds doubtful all around), but letting Maggie slide, even temporarily, is far away from anyplace that Zipper is likely to be.

Maggie, quickly recovering her composure and instinctively channeling her consternation into aggression, retorts, "I'm sure you know all about dirt that doesn't wash off," missing the point. "No reason for you to wait for me to finish, Zipper. I don't have any money for you."

Zipper doesn't talk, doesn't leave; rather, she closes the bathroom door, and the steam becomes a third presence.

Growing a little uneasy, Maggie affects a tone that is observational and distracted and tries, "Poor William must really be broke—I've never seen so much come. You know, Zipper, if you're not going to handle him gratis, you really ought to teach him to jerk off regularly."

Zipper is now ready to speak, but it is with some effort that she keeps her voice under control. "What you did was not right," she says.

"What I did!" Maggie turns off the shower and throws open the door. Neither woman acknowledges her nakedness as she rips a towel from the rack and indignantly dries her hair. Feigned laughter: "I wasn't the only one who did. How dare you! How do you know it was even my idea? You weren't even there. This whole thing is none of your fucking business!"

"Not even you could believe that, Maggie. And I do not care what happened or who helped you. You knew it was wrong, and you still did it."

"I'm not listening to this," says Maggie, wrapping the towel around herself. "Get the fuck out of my room!" Angrily she steps out of the shower stall and starts to push past Zipper.

But Zipper, in a defensive move that is partially reflexive and partially deliberate, spins on the taller woman, and with a fistful of red hair, slams her face against the bathroom wall—cop style.

Not expecting or interested in pursuing a fight, but not rolling over either, Maggie remains motionless and says, "This is nice. Did you learn this at your last gang bang when bachelor number seventeen tried to stiff you?"

Her pluck impresses Zipper, who says in her ear, "Never again," before releasing her and walking from her room.

Years ago (this story is not part of my ice cube/tea leaf trick; it was related to me by Zipper shortly after we first met as part of our mutually effusive explanations of ourselves) Zipper was working in a cathouse in a nasty part of some city—she didn't tell me where, only that it was not in the United States—when she ran into some trouble with one of her tricks. From what she told me, the place was nothing more than a corrugated iron shack—one big room, set up with bed-sheet partitions strung on sagging ropes from wall to wall. The clientele would then choose their girl simply by pulling back a sheet-curtain and taking a look, whether or not the girl was occupied at that particular moment. This allowed the girls to remain in their places at all times, rather than losing themselves in idle gossip or otherwise unprofitable activities—a situation, I gathered, insisted on by the two aging sisters who ran the place. All in all, a very charming little establishment.

So, one evening Zipper was alone in her room when she was visited by a badly-dressed-but-has-some-money local. The guy wanted a blow job, and he dropped his pants and climbed onto the cot. Zipper went to work—this, she explained, was no picnic, as the guy was in dire need of a bath—but two minutes into it, she felt his hands closing on her throat, so tightly that she could not even yelp. Just then, his hands still on her neck—and this is when it began to make sense to her—he came right into her mouth, now open wide and gasping for air. Zipper, being young at the time and somewhat opportunistic, seized the moment and bit down hard while simultaneously grabbing his testicles in a fist of fury.

This is where she checked out of the scene, for evidently the hapless trick struck her quite a blow to the head and thus got the full attention of Zipper's already suspicious coworkers. Some twenty minutes later she awakened in the far corner of the house to the gentle but insistent prodding of the woman who served as the house medical adviser. Zipper was given her week's pay, as well as strong encouragement to leave the local jurisdiction posthaste. Later she learned that the trick, though still in one piece, had nonetheless gone on an uncontrollable rampage in the house, smashing, tearing, and threatening everything in sight. Another customer, who happened to be on the scene and was none too happy about the interruption, took it upon himself to quiet things down by shooting the wild man dead through the heart. This man was also asked to leave, and while neither expulsion seemed just to Zipper, the whole episode did, she claims, teach her how to better roll with the punches.

Now my ice, waning but fighting the good fight, rolls along the curve of my glass; without hesitation, accelerating in keeping with the appropriate physical laws, Zipper walks the convex hallway from Maggie's room to my deck. I am not there at the moment; I am still here in the big room. It is Laurie whom Zipper finds on the deck this early afternoon, and it is Laurie whom she expected to find.

"I see you like the sun here too," says Zipper amicably—and it is absolutely genuine, for she is far more capable of sudden mood shifts than she is of insincerity.

In a playful challenge—testing the water—Laurie responds, "What else have you seen that I like?"

"I am sorry. I mean to say that I like the sun, also."

Laurie continues, "In that case, what else is there here that you like?"

"I don't understand," says Zipper, but I'm sure she does and is simply testing the water for herself by playing the *I have little English* part. "I mean that both of us enjoy the sun. Is that right?"

"Well, I can only speak for myself. Have a seat; it is rather pleasant out here."

If not pleasant, then something. It is something out there. It is really, really something out there. Out there in the bright and harsh sunlight, warm, true, and strong of contrast; out there where now must transpire myriad communications and myriad communication; out there, now beyond even THEIR control, much less mine. Here I sit, making random guesses as I suck out of random glasses—my worst only a breath away from my best—a far fucking cry from the rap on the deck. Out there the talk is sublime—or, if not the talk, then at least the talking— still transcending the mere prattle of men anyplace that I've ever been, or that they've ever seen. Random guesses: I am and will always: filled with wonder and reverence: that which never stops communicating: their worst word holds a thousand times more meaning than my best guessed word-geste.

Zipper graciously takes a chaise—the one I had been sitting on earlier, during our discussion—and rotates it toward the sun, parallel with Laurie's. My regular chaise, my sleeping chaise, sits empty and askew between the two women.

"I'm lucky," she starts. "I always have time for the sun. Before, working mostly at night, I spent most of my days on the beach, and here there is no work; there is only this wonderful patio."

"You're also lucky to have such dark skin," says Laurie. "I bet you never burn. I'm a slave to my lotion. Even then, after all this hard work [an ironic sweeping of her languid arm], all this hard work, I lose my tan almost as soon as I get it." She clamps her mouth shut in self-deprecating sarcasm: see what hell my life is!

Now armed with the pretext of acknowledging this common experience, the women look briefly into each other's eyes, both searching for the next foothold, a clue to the next level, directions to the next, deeper meeting place. They smile, linger a slender beat too long, but it's okay; they can do this.

Zipper breaks first, but only because she is able to get more, faster than the younger Laurie. Eyeing the water, she asks, "Do you swim?"

"No, I don't know how," says Laurie. "In fact, I don't even like to get wet. I bathe, of course. But even that was hell for me as a kid, and I can't say that I relish it now. I just don't like the feeling of water—of being covered with water. Even a shower sort of bugs me. Maybe I'm an anachronism: the ancient Greeks stayed away from the water, also."

"Are you Greek?" says Zipper, who sees in herself a bit of atavism.

"No, not at all," says Laurie, chuckling at the oversimplification. "I think my troubles are more profound," but seeing Zipper frown, she adds quickly, "Not that I would mind being Greek—I don't know if you're Greek—I mean more profound than a bad-penny gene. I mean that if I'm fucked up it begins and ends with me; it's not something we can put down to my ancestry . . . How the hell did we get on this?" She is suddenly a little uncomfortable, hearing her own remarks and realizing that she has been unguardedly discussing herself. Laurie is a person who prefers to use conversation as an opportunity to bring out the details of others. For her it is a natural defense and comes effortlessly, and while she did expect more of an exchange during this talk with Zipper, she is alarmed to have lost the advantage so quickly.

Zipper, though, in her demeanor seems unaware of any gain. "No, I am not Greek. But I think that you are too hard on yourself. Why do you say that your troubles are profound?" She leans slightly toward Laurie, really wanting to hear her answer, actually interested in what words will be spoken. She is prepared to empathize, and this may be as catty as Zipper gets.

"Oh, I didn't really mean it. I was just talking."

"Then why are you here? Can you see that this is not a place for healthy people?"

Laurie, digesting this, says nothing for a moment. Finally: "There are some things in my past, and I am looking at them. You know, I just sort of landed here after that party, and now I'm using this time here as a break to . . . to take a look at myself." And with a little exasperation, directed not so much at Zipper as to herself, she says, "What is it you want me to tell you? Yes, I have some personal problems. You don't?"

Addressing her by name for the first time, Zipper says, "Laurie, I do not want you to talk about things that are private to you. If there is something in your past—whatever it is you are thinking about—then that is not my concern. I feel there are things about us that are alike." A deliberating beat, then: "I am sorry, but I think you are here on purpose. I think you came to that party because you knew where it was."

Laurie looks around. They are alone on the deck, the doors closed. "Can we leave it at that then—at least for now?"

Zipper, by way of answering, doesn't answer at all. "You are friends with William?" she says.

"No, you are friends with William. I just met him." Normally this sort of question would worry her, but she is pleasantly surprised that Zipper took her cue so willingly; in fact, Laurie is feeling a spark of camaraderie and finding it a welcome change, despite herself.

"Well," says Zipper with emphasis, exaggerating for effect her characteristically stepped delivery, "he is a good person. He is someone you should know better. I think that he is interested in you."

Laurie smiles, Zipper almost does, and yet another level is reached. Rising, Laurie moves closer. She abandons her lounge in favor the one nearest Zipper, my sleeping chaise. After first rotating it to suit her purposes—presumably her tan—Laurie settles into it, adjusting her ass, getting her bearings, finding a way to talk to Zipper.

Sitting now closer, under the sun and in light of a hitherto unsuspected meeting place, Laurie says, "He's not without charm, and I suppose something of the sadness in him is appealing." She picks a bottle of baby oil out of a nearby bundle of such things. "I was under the impression that you two were . . . affiliated," she says, pouring off some oil into her hand and spreading it over her arms and shoulders, the backs of her legs. "Or am I getting you confused with Double Felix?"

Zipper snickers at this. "I know what you mean. They are not sleeping together, but they act like they want to be." She is looking at the oil and its application as if witnessing the procedure for the first time. "This protects you from the sun?" she asks.

Laurie pauses. "You've never used baby oil?"

"Oh yes, but never outside like this."

"Actually, I don't know what the hell it's supposed to do—give me a deeper, darker tan, I think. I just do it because I always have," she confesses.

Zipper continues. "But no, please. William and I are just . . . close. He was my first friend here. You should get to know him. Maybe you can even get him to leave the house for . . . [tossing her hair from her shoulder] you know, for a night."

"What do you mean?" says Laurie, laughing and politely failing to address the nuance. "When was the last time he went out?"

"He just likes it here. He hates to go down the hill."

Laurie decides to let this sit. Putting down the oil, she scoots around on the chaise and tinkers with its back, finally dropping it to a more re-clined position. She balls up a towel for a pillow and mounts the lounge, facedown in order to sun her back. Her face is now away from Zipper, and she says, "I don't mean to be rude, but I can't seem to turn my head that way when I lie on my stomach. We can still talk though. Anyway, I never do my back for very long."

"Would you like some of your oil on your back?" says Zipper.

"Hey, that'd be great. You better be sure you don't mind getting it on your hands though. It's hell to wash off."

Sitting up on the edge of her chaise, Zipper pours some oil and applies it efficiently to Laurie's back. She is thorough, but her fingers do not linger. When she is done she wipes her hands on her own legs and lies back on her chaise. "You have very pretty skin," she says, "very young." Matter-of-factly: "You have the attention of all the men in this house, Laurie."

But Laurie already knows this. She also knows that Zipper knows she knows this, and thus sees no need to respond. Nor does she offer to apply oil to Zipper, for Zipper would decline, and they both know this.

It is not quite two o'clock, and the afternoon sun covers them evenly and indifferently; that is probably what they dig about it.

But from where I sit—drunk and still alone in the big room, the big, dark room—the sun's got a great gig. I pour more gin and think about it. Oh yes. Yes, yes, yes: I reflect on it, big in the sky and ubiquitous in the air. Its fucking long rays shoot down and wantonly caress their firm tits, their hot little asses.

CHAPTER SIX

So I am left with yet another pensive afternoon in the big room: my bottles, my glasses, all of Double Felix's great stuff, and me, heretofore alone and uninterrupted by Zipper or Maggie, Laurie or . . . Timmy. She must know. Of course she knows. So why didn't she mention it? Hell, she completely dismissed it! I hate that! Why am I always so fucking obvious to everyone, a fucking open book? I just got here, and I've already been here too long. I think it might be time . . . to leave this fucking place. Four months of sitting around is enough; and when a great piece finally does show up and I tag it, she turns out to be as goofy as the rest. Fucking Laurie. Barely has time to talk to me since I brought her home this morning, but plenty of time for Bill or his girlfriend. Plenty of time for any fuck-up that happens to be lying around.

THWOKKK

What is it with chicks and losers? Why does every drooling, bag-toting drunkard with his hands in his underwear attract girls like he's flypaper? It's not as if I didn't rack her to within an inch of her life last night; it's not as if she has anything to complain about.

THWOKKK

Bill didn't—probably couldn't—nail her, so where's the attraction? Nowhere, that's where. It's this stupid thing that chicks do to piss US off. They're embarrassed or something. They hate the way WE can make them feel good. They hate the way they need US. So they make like it's nothing and take their revenge by hanging out with deadbeats, geeks, or fags.

THWOKKK

Laurie spends the day moping around and wasting time with Bill not because she wants to, but because she knows that it'll bug me. It's just part of her hang-up; she figures anything's better than letting me have the upper hand. She figures I'm way too together, and that she'll never be able to control me.

THWOKKK

Maybe it isn't just here, but it sure is especially here. What it's been since I got here—oh, sure, it's been fun and full of beer and pussy—what it's been is drag city. It's been like I'm not part of it, and that doesn't make any sense cause I'm always part of it, and when the competition is cripples, then I'm always, always part of it.

THWOKKK

And no matter what she wants to waste her time with, I sure was part of Laurie last night. I sure was.

THWOKKK

This time here, all this time here is just about good for nothing. No one to shoot hoop. No one to play anything and never enough guys for a team anyway . . . so what good's the place if you can't use it?

THWOKKK

It's not like I didn't try. At first I was such a fucking go-along that it makes me want to puke to remember it. Drinking in the morning. Watching TV. Watching everybody look at everybody else.

THWOKKK

Watching everybody look at me.

THWOKKK

Listening to long boring jokes that don't make you laugh. Eating. Not eating. The fucking . . . that's okay, but here no one really has much fun doing it.

THWOKKK

Once I saw two fags go into the same room during a party. I wanted to fuck them up—but it's not my house. I hate that. I should've fucked them up anyway. I don't need that kind of disgusting faggery in my face—keep it private. That was a big party. What if someone wanted to use that room for a real fuck? Those guys were lucky they didn't get in my way.

THWOKKK

I should've fucked those fags up.

THWOKKK

Another time I spent forty minutes trying to make this foxy little thing that was staying over after a party. Then I find out she's a dyke! A fucking dyke! She was beautiful!

THWOKKK

She was beautiful, and I'm trying to make her, and she's a dyke! I could see it if she was ugly or old, but she was cute and my age. What a fucking waste.

THWOKKK

Just like this whole place, she was a fucking waste.

THWOKKK

THWOKKK

THWOKKK

I can do this for hours—it's sport. Everybody does it, at least everybody that I'd spend time with. But do you think I could interest just one single deadbeat to toss a ball around with me? In four whole months? Just once? No fucking way.

THWOKKK

Me and the wall. I throw it, it comes back.

THWOKKK

Free beer is nice, but enough is enough.

THWOKKK

It's not like I'm getting any more pussy here than I could on any night in the marina. It's not like I can't go back to the firm.

THWOKKK

They told me anytime. Clear my head. There'll be plenty of litigation to go around whenever I'm ready. Always plenty of litigation.

THWOKKK

Maybe chill for a week at home first. Maybe call Mom when I get down the hill—not from here.

THWOKKK

Fuck her. Let her hang out here with the deadbeats. I can't say goodbye to everyone. If she misses me then she misses me. I don't owe her anything.

THWOKKK

I don't owe anyone here anything. I could just split right now and not tell anybody.

THWOKKK

I could just go to my room, get my stuff, and hike down the hill. If someone asks what I'm doing, then fine, I'll say goodbye. If no one notices, then that's fine too.

THWOKKK

But I'm sure not busting my ass looking for anybody. I'm sure not about to paw at Felix's door just to say bye. He probably doesn't even remember my name.

THWOKKK

Fuck him for wasting my time.

THWOKKK

It's not like I spent eight years in school so I could learn to sit around here and jack off. It's not like this is the sort of return that the folks are looking for—not after the investment they made.

THWOKKK

Freaky chicks. Fags. Drunks. Enough is enough. I don't belong here.

THWOKKK

It's sure not like I belong here. It's sure not.

THWOKKK

THWOKKK

THWOKKK

CHAPTER SEVEN

... **Timmy. But I speak too soon,** for as announced to me by the concentric ripples on the surface of my drink, the front door has opened and is even now being slammed. I turn—my own afternoon version of quickly—on my barstool and find myself face to ass with the Sport himself, Timmy, bending over to retrieve his dropped ball.

Standing and about-facing, he catches himself on a strange little feminine gasp. Evidently he did not expect to find me here. "Billy!" he says, remembering to grin. "How's yours hangin'?"

Absently I look down at it, but my view is obscured by my pants. I attempt to sense it, to feel how it is hanging, but this proves surprisingly difficult, and I wonder if alcohol has benumbed me or if indeed there really is something wrong with it.

"I'm not sure," I answer truthfully, and not without some concern. "How is yours hanging?"

"Yeah." Timmy's eyes go wide, his cheeks inflate, shoulders shrug: how 'bout that? "Well, I gotta go to my room for a minute," he says, looking at me hopefully.

"By all means. Don't let me hold you up."

He doesn't, and I return to my drink.

I bet Timmy loves this place. I bet he'll retire here, be around for a million years after I'm gone. Free beer, women—of course he loves it.

Women tend to like him too, though to me he has always been pretty much a supernumerary, a spare pea in the pod. I remember when I first met him. He asked me something about the Lakers—basketball, I think—and was gravely disappointed when I had nothing to say on the subject. In fact, that's about what I said. He asked me who I liked on the Lakers, and I said, "Basketball . . . right?" He looked confused for a minute; he was probably waiting for me to crack a smile and confess that professional basketball was my life. But when he saw that I really was uncertain about which ball it was that the Lakers tossed around, he looked over my shoulder, told me that it had been nice talking with me, and walked away.

Timmy is many things I could never and would never be. He is not at all disturbed by himself. He is always satisfied with the first available answer to any question that he inadvertently stumbles over. He is the sort of man who a woman in her waning twenties might marry. A match made in a 7-Eleven, she there for milk, he for a microwave burrito. He might grunt on his way out the door, bewailing a forgotten Slurpee through bean-caked lips. She would be at first surprised that he had spoken to her, then perhaps smitten, and, in a rush of maternal response, run back for the melting Slurpee while Timmy holds the door open and the Iranian clerk in the red and white smock wishes he had access to the air-conditioning switch. Months later and none too soon, the broken bride would stand at the altar wearing a most unnatural color. I could do much worse, she would think to herself from behind her tears and veil, the Carpenters blowing off the organ, her cousin on video.

"Well, Billy, I'm gonna take off."

This time it is he who has startled me. I was not prepared for such a literal interpretation of "for a minute," and I jump on my stool, spinning around so hard that I practically make a full revolution. The move though is too slapstick for Timmy to appreciate, and while I am ready to begin laughing with him at myself, his face does not split into a smile.

"What?" I say, realizing that he is trying to communicate to me something of consequence. I notice that he carries an overstuffed purple and yellow gym bag, replete with red and black–banded sweat sock dangling halfway out of a torn zipper as if, finally at wit's end with the general Timminess of its surroundings, it has gathered its courage and is preparing to jump.

"I'm leaving. I got my stuff—this is all of it—and I'm gonna split." But he doesn't move, and I get the impression that he is waiting for me to challenge him.

"For a few days?" I say, working hard to get this all down. I remain in position—no mental energy to spare on motor functions—and I think I feel the barstool beginning to tip.

"No. No, I'm going for good, Billy. I guess things around here are just moving too fast for me. Anyway, I think it's time to get my life going again; you know, back to work and . . . and all that." This out, he straightens his back and takes a breath: poised for final departure. "Can I count on you to take care of the women for me?" he asks cheerfully.

I see that Timmy is being nice, that now—for at least this one moment—he likes me. It is a function of farewell. I too remember liking people best at the moment of separation, to the point of reevaluating previously held opinions, ingrained though they may have been. So it is now with my feeling toward Timmy. His simple remark of chumminess is exactly the kind of trite nicety that sparks wildfires of smarmy effusion. But I am in no condition to follow such a road this afternoon, at least not physically. Instead I remain on my barstool and wink at him. If he were a whore whom I had just ejaculated in, I would be hugging him cheek to cheek. I used to do that; after fucking a hooker I used to put my face next to hers and hold her, love her.

But Timmy, like those many women, is growing impatient. He is wondering what his obligation is, what price this barter of affection brings.

My barstool remains steady as it settles back into the perpendicular. "Sure, Timmy," I say. And taking a cue from our common maleness, I add, "You won't be saying goodbye then? Not even to . . . anybody?"

"Naw." He says it abruptly, cutting off what should be the lingering aaawww. As he makes his way to the door he has certain trappings of a man doing what he wishes to do—most noticeably a forward look. Timmy never had much respect for the doorknob on this door; he always tried pushing hard and quick, before dropping his hand a few inches and turning; in fact there is a worn spot in the paint, smudged and unctuous from this repeated contact. Often I wondered whether he really forgot that use of the knob was required, or just did this out of habit, perhaps a small act of civil disobedience from a solidly obedient civilian. True to form on this final occasion, he hits the door hard with his hand, and though I would give a lot to have it yield in an inanimate yet poetic gesture, it merely rattles as it always does—always did.

So it is up to me to be the poet. "Where's the aaawww, Timmy?" I yell after him. Truly the sort of remark that I in my stupor always make, it is exactly what is required here to remind us of our dislike for each other.

But he betters me. "Yeah, right," he says, and I can tell that he neither heard nor cares to have heard. "Take care, Billy." This latter is muffled, for he is already out the door, which closes behind him.

There is, loud and fast, the hyperactive ticking of my watch. Stainless steel, mechanical, Swiss, it chatters from my wrist to my ear, a distance of perhaps three inches. I open my eyes; my head is on the bar; I have been asleep. This watch will long outlive me, but for now it is only three o'clock.

I feel bad—and good. That is to say I am salvageable. This nap, unplanned though it may have been, turned out to be of exactly the right duration. I am sobering and groggy, and near what will be my second wind. Knowing what I need, I grab a bottle of bourbon from the bar—around the neck, the coolest and most useless way to hold a fifth—and lumber off my barstool. (Amazingly, I failed to fall off while I slept—a rude awakening I have experienced more than once at this very bar.) On my left is one of two doors that lead to the kitchen. It's an industrial-type swinging door, but without the usual portholelike window through which one can see outgoing traffic and so avoid collision. During catered parties this has proved treacherous, and I normally eschew this entrance and thus the kitchen altogether, the other door being the location of the only confirmed cockroach sighting in the history of the house—a surefire place for me to find the willies.

Today I make an exception and boldly, bodily bust through the door, slamming it against a stainless steel rack laden with cast-iron pots and pans. The noise, though somewhat deafening, is par for my course, and it is not until the denser din dies and a gargantuan ladle rocking once too often on its shallow hook falls to the black-and-white tile floor with a solitary thud that I shriek, jump, and almost drop the bourbon bottle. Sweat and silence thus broken, I try to compose myself and immediately vomit in the great shiny sink.

Thus fortuitously prepared, I make myself a pot of rabidly black coffee. Into an oversized beer mug filled with ice I then pour the coffee, burned and virulent, while doing likewise with the bourbon, half and half. The ice, melting on contact, permits me to chug down the slop in short order—no doubt an advisable procedure—and so I am spared most of the actual flavor. Even so I hold my nose, my left arm comically draped in an arch before my eyes, and squint hard, for this often helps as well.

Amidst the stained and stainless, the alloy and aluminum, the altogether charred, chipped, and polished condition of Double Felix's overly equipped food factory, I feel obliquely threatened, and much at home. Standing here imbibing my vile potion and waiting for what may come, I am at the mercy of the dinosaurs of decoction that surround me. There are sizes and shapes which defy description, let alone application, monstrous pieces of work no doubt wrought by men clad in bearskins and sandals who were fearful of such newly conceived and therefore cursed proceedings yet carried on, anxiously awaiting the time that they might turn over the finished product to the facile handling of the village women, fearless, prescient, and much better equipped to keep in check the ossified giants. Looming high on the top shelf of a wrought iron throne to my right is an enormous cauldron, big enough to conceal a man—perhaps a too-good-at-his-job African explorer. Made out of god knows what, it looks to weigh over a hundred pounds, and while I realize that such a thing has some specialized contemporary uses, I am more comfortable thinking of it as an anachronism, maybe brimming over with stone soup for scores of battle-weary medievals, or performing some function in an arcane and hitherto uncovered ritual of colonial Salem. Like me this pot has never had much purpose here in the society of modern-day men. It takes up space. No one could ever imagine using it, but neither could they imagine discarding it. It is interesting to look at—for a while; then it grows annoying in its inactivity. I have no doubt that generations have been born and died waiting to find a use for such

have nothing to say. "Laurie?" I say, though I haven't a clue what I will add when she responds.

"Huh," she says, grateful that I have taken on the burden of speech.

Showtime. I fix a pensive look, as if what I am about to say is so important that I must be careful to word it properly. I'm sure I am fooling no one. Precious seconds tick by; she eagerly awaits my words. What pearl will fall from my lips? What the hell happened to the repartee? It has been my experience that when conversation gets this difficult it usually indicates a deeper tension or unease, a fresh preoccupation with the intimate. I can stall no longer, so I bail out with my last resort held tightly in my arms, to be fastened around my back on the way down.

I release a breath and say, "You didn't know Timmy had left. You heard the news from me just now, and you didn't want me to think that he snuck out on you. Right? I'm right, aren't I?"

Now that it's out, I am rather proud of this, composed, as it was, under such tight and difficult conditions. But Laurie seems unimpressed; in fact, her face melts down to an expression of exasperated ennui, such as might be worn by an air passenger who has just learned of yet another in a long series of flight delays.

"William," she says, "in the interest of making a little headway, and if you can stand the candor, and if you promise not to respond to this in any way [I nod, probably too vigorously], I will tell you something that I normally wouldn't." Reluctant but resigned, she continues, "I don't give a fuck about Timmy. That may sound like a bitter woman, but it's not; it's literally true. I do not care about Timmy now, any more than I did when I was fucking him."

Glad I am, is my first thought, that we have mutually precluded a response from me, for there are many things here that I need to address in my own mind, such as a little headway . . . toward what? To what end are we interested in making a little headway? Why do I once again find myself at the receiving end of some greater plan, authored, as usual, by a woman? Perhaps I am a vacuum, vacuous to such a degree that I cry out for manipulation. And why wouldn't I be able to stand the candor? More to the point, if it is understood that I am not up to the candor, then why the hell am I being subjected to it now? Why do I suddenly find myself resentful, as if the truth, any truth—good news, bad news—any truth, is punishment? What's in it for me, this brass-tacks Timmy report? Why should I be so informed? There's a strange, growing panic in me. Having made a simple and trite remark, solely to cultivate the friendly progression of a conversation, I suddenly find myself on the business end of a real communication, one to which I may not respond! I feel like I just dropped a quarter into a beggar's cup, only to have my wrist grabbed and pulled. I feel like I'm not only out of my league, but have just been informed of the fact. It all makes me pine, momentarily, for Zipper. She would never play such a dirty trick. Or if she did, she would at least work around me somehow, instead of making me an accomplice in my own undoing. She knows that I prefer to pilot those flights solo.

"What time is it?" I ask.

Picking up my wrist, Laurie looks at my watch. "Almost three thirty," she says, and though she lets my wrist fall under its own weight, she follows through with her hand, keeping in contact and remaining so to the point of making it a gesture.

There might be a tiny spark here, but even if there is, it might also be merely a flash. Jaded temporarily as a result of my earlier experience with Maggie, it is the nature of the beast to rigorously investigate all such leads. I directly flip my hand so that the wrist is up. We are passively engaged in something of a wrestler's grip, our wrists touching, our fingers diffident. I am that beast.

Trying unsuccessfully to lift one eyebrow with a meaningful flair—a trick I have always wanted to master, but alas, I stand too far from my simian ancestors—I ask, "Where is everybody?"

"Timmy, as you have just reported, is history. Double Felix is holed up in his room. And Maggie went down the hill; I don't know what for." Her hand, while still in contact, is motionless. This is apparently where she wants to be for now, no hither, no thither.

"What about Zipper?" Endeavoring not to add a random and relative motion, I keep my hand frozen under hers. I dare not move it lest I cross a signal, manufacture or nullify one.

"I don't know. I was on the deck with her earlier. I left her there, but when I looked out later she was gone. I don't know where Zipper is." The hand, the grip, delicate, faint, definitely hither. "She's somewhere. She's not here."

But something tells me that Zipper is indeed here, at least in some immeasurable degree. Or do I just want her to be here so that she might enrich my action and feelings with her extraordinary cues, modify my behavior and witness the result, absolve me of all responsibility, up to and including the responsibilities of recollection, assimilation, digestion? I wish that I were older, Laurie younger; I wish that Laurie were my daughter, for as such she could endow this day with the means to make cogent my pariahdom.

I relax my hand; she tightens her grip. I am a woman. I want Laurie to make me, and I know that she is up to it. "You're so . . . so intimidating," I say, my penis rising up and away from me.

Laurie swivels her torso to me—diagonally, the line of travel skew—and gets me down with my back on the couch. I am between her knees, under her arms, pinned down and tickled by her hair as it plays teasingly over my face.

"I think you like to be intimidated," she says as she unbuttons my shirt. "But what is it really, William?" She pauses, struggling over a difficult button—though from her angle they must all be somewhat difficult. "What is it really that you like about me?"

"I don't know . . . Somehow you seem like something that I should do."

"But then, who doesn't—right?" she says, laughing, releasing the button.

"But then, who doesn't—right. What I mean is I feel an attraction toward you that transcends the usual checklist of qualifications," I say.

"In other words, I don't have the usual qualifications." Her hands, now inside my open shirt, caress firmly my chest in the practiced manner of a masseur. Up and inward she pulls, as if to squeeze my breath away; then she rubs in reverse, and I am inhaled.

"Oh, you have them. You know you have them. But they're beside the point, see. My point is that they're beside the point," I say in a virtual purr. Her touch is wonderful. I feel like swooning, for chrissake.

"They're never beside the point," she says. "Tell them to me. Tell me my qualifications." She has her fingers on my nipples, and the sensation is not especially pleasant.

"Not my cup of tea," I say parenthetically, indicating her increasingly aggressive pinches.

"Sorry." She retreats to my shoulders.

"You're beautiful . . ."

"Too general. What about me is beautiful?"

"Your hair." By way of demonstration, I tangle my fingers in her hair.

"Stop. I'll never get a comb through it. Hair's too easy, what else?"

"Sorry. But now that you mention it, that's what I like about your hair: the way it's always . . . disheveled."

"Yeah, yeah. What else?"

"Your breasts," I answer, and I begin to worry her buttons.

"Too lecherous. What else?" she says, but lets me continue with her shirt.

"Your breath."

"Better than yours, Jack Daniel," she laughs.

"No, actually I'm a Wild Turkey."

"Whatever. Come on. What is it about me that drives you wild? What is it really?"

My hands are now in her shirt. Her breasts are firm, supple, receptive to my touch. I open her shirt and see that they are truly pretty things; in fact, above all they are just that—pretty things. It seems that right now, being caressed under my hungry hands, they are serving their one true purpose. It's as if, assigned the maternal duty of giving milk, they would turn away and sneer incredulously: NO WAY! That is not their destiny, and I am certain that this girl will never bear children. The thought endears her to me. I have always considered the concept of procreation to be somewhat anachronistic, at least insofar as it is considered a virtual requirement of maturity. Children, fatherhood— for me these things have no place; indeed, the reality of a scion would amount to nothing more than just another loose end in my life; worse, for it would extend beyond my life, beyond my control.

The days of my past, what I had then, what passed for an acceptable life in the eyes of my family, were littered with relics of ancestry. Inscribed books, antique lamps, world war trappings, et cetera, all came to me as a premature inheritance, a desperate effort by my parents and their parents to will progeny from me, the youngest and last best hope out of a small litter of aging, effectually barren disappointments. Even after it became clear that there were to be no grandchildren—great or otherwise—forthcoming, and that my thinking was pretty much the final-generation thinking of my siblings; even after my life became unacceptable by their hearty Midwestern standards, still came the cherished objects, still came the once and finite heirlooms. Eventually I called, put a stop to it. "What will you do with Grandpa Paul's spectacle collection?" asked my father precipitously in response to my impending addressee-unknown status. I'm a cold son of a bitch. I promised to ship everything back; in reality it all sits in a chain-link storage locker in Tustin, California, awaiting its destiny, an earthquake, perhaps a misguided probate borne of an interstate technicality, or a selling-off for recovery of unpaid storage fees. I don't care. I hate the stuff, the shackling.

"It's cause you're young, Laurie. That's why I want to touch you so intensely—because you're young."

And she smiles, sits up and pulls off her shirt, and leaning back down, offers to my mouth a nipple.

Soft, new to my tongue, there it hardens. Her body waxes and grows ruddy as she releases herself to me, and we charge down the familiar path. We are naked. We know each other better now. We are gentle and utterly devoid of the pique that flitted over our earlier encounters. But even as her body rises and falls on me, I realize—and I think Laurie does too—that this is not and will never be our relationship, that the real quality between her and me is yet to be discovered, exists in a different, more personal arena.

Then, inexplicably, I lose my erection. It just vanishes. Well within her, nearing conclusion, it is simply gone, and gone abruptly. Laurie feels it and looks at me oddly startled, as if what has just happened is quite new to her experience: Did you come? I look back, just as bewildered: no.

"I . . . I don't know," I say. "I was fine, and then . . . then it just died." And in a misguided attempt at salvaging some pride, I add, "Hell, Laurie, I was even afraid that I would come before you," thinking of Maggie, despite myself.

But fortunately she disregards this latter, and I can see that she is moving inside of herself, thinking of something that has absolutely nothing to do with me.

We lie quietly, me still more or less inside of her, her now lowered to my chest, her head nestled by my neck. She begins to sob. It comes in waves. I don't know why Laurie is crying, but I knew that she would. I also know that these tears of hers are for her eyes only. They are so deeply private, so much a part of her alone, that I dare not consider from whence they came. This is my gift to her, but she will never know of it.

Rather, I turn my thoughts to what has just happened, for outcome notwithstanding, this little union has given me over to a refreshing self-satisfaction. This situation could have, perhaps, more readily fulfilled its promise right at the beginning—specifically, at the moment it became clear to me that Laurie was entertaining sexual thoughts of me. Had Zipper walked in on us when Laurie and I were just starting to play touchie-feelie with our hands, thus ending the thing right there, then I think I would have had something quite neat. But through some cosmic and passive failing on Zipper's part, that did not happen. Being what I am, however, I will take the thing as if it held that value; I will accept that, the high-water mark, as the average depth. I do this at the risk of—no, with the certainty of—appearing blatantly male. This is how I can glean an A+ from Laurie, at least for my purposes. This is how it

must be for dogs, why they can keep such a positive attitude. Like cam-
els with their water, dogs must have a way of ferreting out tiny pockets
of affection encountered along the way, and saving said pockets, stor-
ing, rationing, digesting only what is and when necessary, making do
with whatever emotional return they get, because dogs, unlike us, have
not lost the wisdom that there are no options . . . save satisfaction.

This is how it is in this universe. This is how the universe holds
our attention. More importantly, this is how the universe keeps us from
checking out, committing no-frills suicide: by keeping the attraction
in the act, not the result. That is, we fuck for the fucking, not for the
babies; they are merely a by-product of what we're really into—or so
it would seem to us. We are not important. Our interest in babies is
not important. The machine runs on stronger stuff, and what is revealed is only what's revealed. Long ago, when I was married, I invariably found that more women flirted with me, or flirted with me more
aggressively, when my wife was present. That was what I needed then.
That was what I required, so that was what I got. I was too young to
handle anything more potent; I still am. In any case it would have been
wrong, would have dealt my wife a hand of injustice, and I've found
that, whenever possible, the universe endeavors to mitigate injustice.
This is what I strive to posit, having grown weary of the orgasm, the
ensuing hand washing. Alone, I have been, at my bathroom sink, my
porcelain lover.

Laurie sleeps now on my shoulder. She is evidently a wizard of
punctuation. The television screens are temporarily inert, no pictures,
no sounds, just alarming reflections of the room, Laurie, myself. Has my
outlook grown darker, or have turned-off TV screens become blacker
over the years? My memories of moon walks and Star Treks, viewed
cross-legged on the floor between my parents (adult and couch-seated,

as I am now) and a Magnavox home entertainment center, include rare periods when that behemoth box was switched to off and sported a screen of olive drab. The screens before me now are virtual black, tech-gray at best, and are so probably better equipped to reflect.

I am reminded of another screen, one from my early twenties. Also off and reflective, it captured and held my attention as well as my image, this time with a different woman resting at my side. I was married at the time, though this girl was not my wife; rather, she was someone whom I had met in a bar on the previous evening—the only time that that classic scenario has ever come to fruition for me—and had grown too fond of with the characteristic alacrity inherent in such affairs. Passionate for a time, we both nervously avoided talk that included the making of plans, and retreated to lovemaking whenever such a conversation seemed imminent. She was right in allowing the relationship to seek its own level, and she brought forth like motivations in me: better hands-off through hands-on.

Painlessly for both of us and to the surprise of neither of us, the girl came quickly to pass, but she left me with that vivid memory, that image of sitting on the couch with her and watching our reflection in a turned-off television. Now facing the same scene, I find that I am feeling those same emotions. Specifically, I have a strange feeling that I have just successfully cheated on my wife. Not my ex-wife, no, the antecedent here is undoubtedly Zipper. This is a bit of a revelation, finding me, as it has, where I least expected it.

Stirring, awake now, Laurie pulls away from me, but only far enough so that she can comfortably speak.

"Well?" she says.

Five o'clock is moments away—quittin' time for me once, in what must have been someone else's life; perhaps I was borrowing it while mine was made ready, fitted.

I remain on the couch. Laurie has repaired to her room for the inevitable freshening-up, and I am left alone with the televisions. Seeking to become temporarily hypnotized by them, I have broken with my own code and turned them all on at once; no sound, just five sets of moving pictures. It's strange, and it smells just a little bit self-abusive. Like some scientifically fictive mind-control device, these cathode-ray tubes seem to be talking to a part of me that is innocent and without defense, and through this unguarded corridor they suck my essence; I will be left a hopeless vegetable, or a vapid zombie-robot in service of some wicked baalistic creature holding the paper on Planet Earth and diabolically bent on foreclosing. I click them all off and am rewarded with a gratifying quintet of electronic fizzles, gasps of disbelief from their puny solid-states. How could I do such a thing? How, indeed.

My erstwhile fantasy approacheth. Strangely, I now recognize her step where earlier I did not. Laurie has that impatience in her gait that is typical of young, pretty women. Not a fast walk, but more of an abrupt walk, as if each step is a disappointment and needs to be forgotten in favor of the next step—new business.

Turning into the room, she stands before me in worn denim and a revealing tee. Despite myself, I have the regrettable thought that she has the mythical just-fucked look; then, on second glance, I am saddened to see that in fact she does have a certain used and weary aspect to her demeanor that I have not noticed before.

"Fully freshened, I trust. You look stunning, as always," I say.

Laurie has a confused look on her face. She was hoping for a cue, and I failed to provide it. Try again, do better. I was about to ask her to pour me some more gin, but now I decide to use the opportunity to hoist my ass and breeze by her. I spit out a quick and casual kiss to her cheek, wanting to be affectionate but not demanding. As a cue, it seems to suffice, for she returns the volley and takes my arm to the bar, where we both sit, this time on the same side.

"I think I'm a little bit embarrassed," she admits as I fill my glass. "I normally wouldn't care . . ." This she lets hang, and I am compelled to provide some sort of adjunct.

But I am temporarily stricken silent, moved that she would choose to be so honest with me. Finally, I say, "It's okay. We just jumped at some bad signals. I can get over it if you can." I smile reassuringly. I'm her father responding to her complaints of a bad day at school.

"Oh, I'll get over it," she says, and of course we both know that this is a relatively small thing, though her tone belies this. "It's just that I think I've behaved . . . ignobly."

"Ignobly?" I say mockingly. Actually, I'm beginning to sense that I may not be the sole concern here—I don't know why, maybe she's raising some little subconscious flag in me—and I want to disguise the fact that I'm just a bit hurt.

But then, maybe ignoble is the perfect word—for me, not her. I think I jumped in her pants too quickly, too recklessly. I think, being older, that I should know better. Most importantly, most potentially ignoble of me, I think it wasn't Laurie who I was trying to fuck, and that's why I couldn't really fuck her. No, rather, I think there's something about Laurie, something that she represents to me, but it is not really her, and this is what I was after. Worse yet, I think I knew it at the time.

"Laurie, look. I fucked up, okay? This is all my fault, not yours. If there's a confession sheet for ignobility to be passed around here, it goes to me. What I'm saying is that I'm not sure that my motives were all that pure." This last, though not completely descriptive of my feelings, is a better choice than trying to explain to a woman whom you've just had sex with that you were really bopping some metaphysical other and not her. What she would hear in such a statement is a far cry from what was said, and what was said is not all that strong of a position to begin with.

She smiles—a bit condescendingly—and says, "Nice try, but I'm afraid that I'm the one who's guilty of ulterior motives."

"What motives?" I say before catching myself. Now I really might be getting hurt.

"It's not important, and I couldn't tell you anyway. Let's just leave things like this: an all-around blanket apology, still pals, but with no further inquiry. Okay?"

So what can I do? I've been out matured—not that that's any great trick. "Okay," I say sheepishly. "Drink?"

From the door: "Good whatever-part-of-the-day-it-is, William and Lady."

And now comes Double Felix, wearing a suit and a tie, and looking very much like a potential litigant. But no, the silk handkerchief puts him in a slightly higher league. This is a man with a tad too much pride and the extra time to spend on it. I know: he reminds me of a retired businessman who, with nothing whatsoever to do all day, still takes the trouble to don the pin-stripe and wing-tips each morning, only to wander around his upscale apartment building chatting with the staff. To them he would be Mr. Ef: small relief from their ennui and a sure-thing sawbuck at Christmas time—goes with the territory.

"Good morning, sire," I say, raising my glass. "Nice outfit; why wasn't I told there was a board meeting this afternoon? Is an introduction in order? Forgive me, but at this point I can't even remember if you two have met or not—Laurie, this is . . ." But my rambling is truncated— and rather abruptly—by Laurie.

"Forgive me for not getting up, but I'm just a little sore. See, I just got off of William. Understand? Double Felix? I got off of him—we were both on the couch, that one there—I got off of him and his dick popped out of me like this . . ." She puts her finger in her mouth and pops her cheek audibly. "So, rather than trouble myself to get up, I'll just sit here and let you come over." She turns back to her drink.

I instinctively look at Double Felix; he appears doleful to say the least. He looks like he'd rather be naked than dressed in that suit, and I don't think I've ever seen him so meaningfully superficial. Though I could have guessed that Laurie was capable of such a splenetic out-burst, I never expected to hear it directed at Double Felix.

Things get pretty quiet sometimes in the big room, and so it is now. The televisions, off, would be no help were they on, for this is drama that surpasses what we've come to expect in drama. No guest aboard *The Love Boat* could handle this—not and sell toothpaste at the same time. No, this is a very personal toothpaste; this toothpaste has been bought, squirted, and spread, and is now circling the drain, unsightly but given to salivary display nonetheless, showing us what we really only wanted to spit out.

"Is this necessary, Laurie?" he says, his voice under a faltering control.

Again I get the impression that this isn't the real show, that the painting I'm looking at is duping me; close examination of these inad-vertent scratches reveal a second, older and more important painting underneath. I would like to melt into the bar and let them finish this on their own. But this private little bar doesn't provide the convenient ref-uge of most bars, and though he is talking to Laurie, I can feel Double Felix's eyes upon me.

"You have betrayed me. I asked for this one thing, and you have betrayed me," he continues, and both Laurie and I wonder after the un-specified antecedent. Did I betray him? Did she? Both of us? It doesn't really matter. It's small potatoes. He's hurt, and we made him that way. I, at least, knew that what we were doing was against his wishes. I be-trayed him, but the word seems now an anachronism, as poetically use-less as the notion behind it.

Dousing the ashes with a squirt of gasoline, I say, "C'mon, you're overdoing it. Is this really such a big deal? So we fucked. So what? You fucked Zipper." This last unfortunately punctuated with a tiny wet burp that comes out of nowhere. I retreat to my glass.

"William, I don't see how that is applicable. Nor do, I think, you. After all, that was the reason she originally came to us, and it was by my invitation. You weren't even interested in meeting her at first. Since then I've always respected your relationship . . . without the benefit of a special request, such as you had from me."

"You knew what the point was," I add. "You engineered it, for chris-sake. You were well aware of the long-term possibilities—probabilities—and you made sure to stick your fingers in right at the onset. Otherwise you would never have been able to tolerate Zipper-plus-William."

Caught up in the momentum of the building argument, I've said a lot more than I ever intended to say about that subject. But the die is cast, something my father used to say at such spilt-milk moments. He also used to frequently remind his eighteen-years-old-and-still-living-at-home son of the well-known edict: as long as you're living in my house you'll abide by my rules. This irrelevant recollection pops into my head with such force that I inadvertently snicker. Habit; this was a surefire way to enrage my dad.

Double Felix is vexed by my remark: a teacher trapped in an end-less string of *but why? but why? but why?* "This is getting us nowhere," he says. "We're touching on issues that are not appropriate for group discussion, and I can see that the trend will only continue in this environment." He is barking orders, but he also has a touch of diffidence in his tone. Pausing to assemble his words, he turns first to me. "William, have another drink and settle down. Come and see me in my room in an hour or so." He looks at Laurie, who still has her back to him, but says nothing, though I'm sure he has something to say. Rather, he leaves the room without further comment.

Looking not exactly communicative, fuming next to me at the bar, Laurie is nonetheless my partner in crime (whosever crime this is), and I feel it is my responsibility to draw her out.

"So," I say, "that was an interesting tack you took there." No reaction. "But I think it worked: I don't think he suspects anything."

She turns to me, stone cold: "I'm sorry to get you mixed up in this," and she gets up and walks out of the room.

I decide to have another drink and settle down before going to see Double Felix in his room. But going I am, whether he's ready for me or not. Let's see: it's almost quarter after five, so I'll go see him at six fifteen, about an hour from now.

Things are not well here, but they have been not well before, and I have every confidence that this is merely a temporary glitch. Maybe Timmy, through his departure and de facto extinction, caused a breach in the brood chain around here, the effects of which have yet to be fully realized. Maggie. I don't know—something indulged in rashly, now a waiting game of digestion. Zipper. Where is Zipper? The very thought of her sends shivers, albeit warm ones, up and down my spine—less down, more up.

I once had a tendency toward humor that was, if not obscure, certainly not readily accessible, and in any event not worth the trip. It looks pretty silly from here, but at the time I never tired of subjecting whomever I was with to these inanities. For instance, if driving with friends and spying an oversized sign with the words PARK HERE and a large arrow, I would find it necessary to say something like: I wonder where we should park? (I was clearly younger than anyone should ever be.) My companions during that period, given sufficient exposure to my jejune remarks, quickly learned to ignore same, as well as, often, their author. I mention this not as a misguided attempt to lament the passing of youth, but because I can see, outside the window and across the driveway, a stray dog asleep in the weeds. I want Zipper here. I want to be able to point to that dog and ask her: do you think we should wake him up? I want to know her reaction.

I'll go and look for her; after all, there's really no reason for me to wait at the bar. I am the master of my own destiny, and I can sure as hell report to Double Felix's door from anyplace in the house. It has become a habit of mine to pause before making any sudden movements, such as standing up from . . . from not standing up. So, having filled my glass for the trip, I commence with the pausing and ready my legs.

Suddenly I am aware that the house is positively silent. There is absolutely no aural evidence that any animate thing occupies this house. For all I hear right now, I could be alone. Even the sounds of my own body elude me. The perennial hum of the world at large: not there. The cumulative buzz of myriad ticks and tocks that drifts into our ears twenty-four hours a day: missing. The orchestration of every noise ever made anywhere, perpetually and reliably amalgamated then distilled down to a back-of-your-head IV of mild distraction in a sucrose base: history.

I do stand. I am in need of a noise. I hit the table with my glass: *bok*.

Not enough—I need a longer noise. I slap myself. Again. Listen: still nothing. I can't possibly be alone here; I know better. Afraid to listen to my watch, much less look at it, my eye instead falls on a remote for one of the televisions. I can't touch it; I am afraid that if I reach for it, I might lose my balance, fall and strike my head, die in this pervading silence. My eyes blur. My bladder burns. It seems a very long time since I last urinated—too long for a living man. Still standing by the bar, I unzip my fly: *zzzip*. I pull out my penis; it seems pitifully small, and I can hold it between my thumb and my forefinger. It takes time, then finally there is liquid. At first a mere dribble trickling along my finger and dripping off the knuckle, it grows in force and becomes a steady stream under pressure which separates from my finger and finds its own path. It hits the floor, fairly quietly at first but soon announcing itself with a rumble as it stakes out its puddle and continues falling upon itself, no longer absorbed by the shocked carpet. It's now loud: *patapatapatapata*. It feels good to hear it. It smells bad, for I have held it too long; nonetheless, it feels good to smell it.

And much to my relief, when the splashing ends, it is replaced by the regular sounds of the house, the city, the rest. I hear water running— plumbed water—in one of the bathrooms. An airplane passes overhead. Probably an antique from Santa Monica airport, for it has that precarious cough that haunts old black-and-white movie soundtracks. Once the bane of inevitably smaller-than-life airmen, it has no doubt become something to be achieved, duplicated, recaptured in its authenticity, like the dying, spitting, last-time-out-before-the-snow-flies sound of a well-tuned Harley. I hear other things. I hear a trillion things, all of them rich and cogent messengers; they sing to me of my continuing sanity. I put my dick back, wipe my hand on my pant leg. Zipper is in her room—I just know it—and I march out of the big room and to her door.

It is closed but not firmly seated against the jamb. Nix the knock—I permit it to swing from my advancing shoulder.

Flooding her room, the sun pours through her westward exposure, vivifying the many colors that she keeps here; I could almost touch them, touch the colors themselves and not merely the objects that carry them. With it comes the sea breeze. Still fresh and pleasant at this late Los Angeles date, it animates the many fluffy, flowing fabrics, the lacy and fringed things that are tossed about in elegant disorder. As with a fugue or a Jackson Pollock painting, there is a method to this matter; I can hear it breathe. Zipper is beyond her open door, languishing on her balcony in apparent ignorance of or indifference to my entrance. I manage the seat at her side, and we both gaze silently out to the water, the very big water.

"Well, I fucked Laurie," I blurt out matter-of-factly, but my words merely establish a midpoint in our stillness. The conversation will begin when Zipper begins it.

From here a pier is visible. Near it is a group of surfer boys (one doesn't see too many surfer girls, or am I just looking in the wrong places?). Evidently this surfing is very important to those who do it, but as with skiing—another big-time time-killer—it is something that holds no appeal for me. These boys out on the water, they will paddle out in their black and green/pink/yellow/blue wet suits, only to manage a stance on the return trip—best-case scenario. Eventually they'll be too old for this fun, this sun. The after-works will turn into one-weekend-a-months, those to beach bar stories and silent moments spent reminisc-ing over a dull and dusty slab of summer, that is the board itself, once a well-waxed hanger of ten now a splintery toe-stubber lurking in the furthest reaches of a Sears Craftsman Utility Storage Shed, which is, after all, more appropriate equipment for a junior VP residing in the

Great Inland Empire. But that will be then; for now, lest boy and board become separated in the surf, the former wears around his ankle a little rubber and Velcro shackle tethered to the latter. I don't really know if skiers employ a similar scheme; I suppose that the solid water in which they play provides a more searchable plenum for wayward rails. I find the whole business annoying, boring and repetitious, tedious—it may as well be basketball. The man in my life whom I disliked the most (a minor character who does not merit proper address) was a skier; he drove a van with a vanity plate to that effect, and he was too old to surf.

Zipper says, "Do you love her?"

"No. I probably did earlier this afternoon, but not now."

"Why? Was it that bad?" This a predictable question: Zipper as a victim of her femininity.

"No, it's not that. You know better than that."

In the surf I see a board pop up and almost become airborne. Its erstwhile rider nowhere in sight, it goes alone to a restless, rocking beaching; nudging the sand as if it would hop out at the slightest sign of welcome. The rider remains hidden in the waves, or maybe I am semi-gin-blind and missing him. In any case, whatever happens down there, I am not a part of it. Even if I were to spring to the phone, infect the proper sandy-blond authorities with my panic, it would mean nothing. The surf-fellows are on the scene, their judgment calls are the ones that count. They alone will determine if life is to be recklessly pursued through foam and algae at the possible expense of sunblock, maybe mousse.

The boy surfaces, laughing.

I say to Zipper, "I can't help but feel that you are more in control of my life right now than I am." Turning to her: "It's comforting. If it's not true, I feel that I could wish it into fact . . . but I also feel guilty."

She starts to respond—at least, she looks at me and opens her mouth—but I interrupt her.

"I wouldn't mind coming home to you. I wouldn't mind working—oh, I don't know—say, in a ketchup factory, screwing the lids on the bottles—just me and ninety-nine machines. I wouldn't mind working in a ketchup factory and coming home to you at night, giving you my pay-check on Fridays. I wouldn't mind it." Suddenly on the edge of my seat, I am caught off guard by my agitation over this quaint little fantasy, and I settle back in my chair.

At once catching and slowing the rhythm, she says skillfully through an upturned corner of her mouth, "I think your check will be in a big brass cash register at our neighborhood bar. And when you are so drunk that you decide to come home, you will give the change to the cocktail waitress who will sneer behind your back at your drunk after kissing your cheek to make sure of the next week's change."

This, of course, is exactly how it would be, and as we laugh together at her rendition, we find ourselves in the midst of our warmest communication of the day.

Turning into the wind, I say, "I suppose I would have to do that for a while, but not forever."

She captures my eyes, and there is meaning in her own. It suddenly occurs to me that I am ready for this, that I'm up for whatever it is she is about to say. I want it. I want it hard and revolutionary. I want it extreme. I want her words to cause me more distress and trouble and work than I ever imagined. But this is too much to ask, and I know that. It is not Zipper's job to make me well; it's mine. Indeed, I am lucky beyond my claim to be close to her, one that understands this so well.

She says, "Do you really think that you will have to do that?"

And since the answer is obvious, since my life, my growth, my love all indicate that I do, I say nothing. Nor does Zipper expect me to respond; rather, she picks up my hand and kisses it. This makes me feel good.

So the sea takes up the slack in the conversation, confidently repeating itself, imparting its wet and recondite lecture freely, and knowing well that we shall never tire of the lesson. Zipper and I are oblivious to the sounds of the house. Were we to listen deliberately, they would still remain beyond our reach. Nonetheless there are sounds. Particularly from Double Felix's bedroom do emanate the sounds of the most profound import, the highest drama, the heaviest of trips. It is a conversation between Double Felix and Laurie. Zipper wouldn't much care, even if she could hear it. I can't hear it—don't even know that it's taking place. But my ignorance won't quell it. It transpires without me, as Zipper and I sit, maybe talk.

Double Felix says, "All right then, it's forgotten. Perhaps I overreacted. In any case, it needn't have any bearing on our future." Catching his own image in a mirror, he adds with a little nod of affirmation, "There mustn't be any limitation on what we shall have together . . . there absolutely must not."

Laurie, seated, chuckles to herself, but it's all noise with no real amusement to back it up. She has decided to affect an attitude of superior indifference—clutched it tightly to her breast as she knocked and walked through his door just moments ago. Her vision, that vision, now grows blurred as the truth of this conversation emerges, wordy fingers playing threateningly at her behind. Her best-laid notions fleeing for higher ground, the vacuum is filling with that affectation, weak though it grows. So the chuckle is young; it makes her sound very young.

"Future?" she says incredulously, though the word was anticipated. "What the fuck are you talking about, future? This is your future, baby.

You're standing in it. This fucking room is the only future you'll ever see!" Almost more . . . then no. Losses are cut. Composure is sought.

"Now Laurie, I've just apologized for my own outburst earlier, so there's really no further reason for you to be upset." Himself now taking a seat, Double Felix crosses his legs at the knees and considers briefly his pant leg, which he gently tugs forthwith. "I think we both know why you're here; for that matter, I think we both always knew that you'd eventually come." His tone is level, paternal, artificially serene. With a glance he confirms the adjusted condition of his pant leg. Okay.

"No. No. I know why I'm here. You know about as much as you did six years ago. I was sixteen—fucking sixteen!—and I was already seeing you. You know what I mean? I was really seeing you. You saw nothing, but I saw you, just like I see you now." Though her tone is level, albeit a bit sardonic, her body is rigid, and her eyes burn with hurt and anger, a visceral passion that cannot be found elsewhere, not even in her lovemaking. A thought flashes in her head, out of place and, stranger still, for the first time: she has slept with men whose names she can no longer remember; moreover, she has slept with men whose names she never knew.

Double Felix is quiet for a time, then he says, "I saw you. I always saw you. You may think that I didn't, possibly because my behavior was not—is not—close to your expectations. Nonetheless, I saw you the whole time. I saw you with real eyes." A true commentary. The man stands, and the pant leg falls.

Double Felix walks to the clear and closed glass doors of his balcony. He and I are separately unaware that our respective eyes are, at this moment, fixed on roughly the same spot on the ocean. But then his attention is gently snagged by a wave running beachward, and he follows it until it breaks against the rocks.

He asks, "Why are you here?"

But Laurie won't accept these terms, this partial surrender. She holds too much forethought, too much premeditated vituperation to allow this scene to mellow. That's not why she came knocking on this door—not yet, not ever.

Shooting forward, sitting upright, but remaining in her chair: "You motherfucker! How dare you try to communicate with me? That's not how this is gonna work. No! You play the imbecile, and I do the talk. I do all the motherfucking talk! That's what I want! That's what's fair."

"Laurie . . ." he starts, still looking at the last known position of the wave, now a memory, yet another promising dissemination begun.

"Fuck you! Fuckyoufuckyoufuckyou! Don't say my name. Don't look at me. Don't think about me." Pausing, she breathes deeply, as if to muster an enormous amount of energy, as if that is what's required to say what she is about to say. "Don't remember me!"

Necessarily disconnecting himself, Double Felix now smiles vaguely. His eyes are still on the water, but he is looking at nothing. "Don't re-member me," he repeats. "I remember you, Laurie. How could I forget you?" Turning to her, he holds open his arms. "Come here, baby. Don't worry: I remember you; I love you. Come here and I'll hold you—you used to love it when I held you. C'mon, baby. Everything will be just fine."

She sees him; silently she sees him standing there, framed by the border of a sliding glass door, bisected with merciless precision by the horizon beyond. And the water seeks its own level, and Double Felix's legs fall on wet blue, his face on space blue, a bit further off and that much more threatening. Laurie now engages in a search of what is and what has been inside of her. This is a time when she would like to be a good girl; indeed, now faced with the imminent conclusion of what she so long strove to conclude, she is predictably uncertain about whether or not to proceed. This is—maybe—a time when she would like to be his good girl.

She sees him; silently she battles the voices in her head. Worse, he is vociferous in his hush, and this adds a tat, making the rat-a-tat seem protracted. It could slide right now; it could slip out of her hands. She remembers a scene she once saw in a movie: a man stating that what he remembered most about stabbing someone in his past was the sound of the knife piercing the victim's flesh. The idea always seemed overly graphic to Laurie, but though she doubts its factuality, she has never given up the image. This is a time when she would like to do better than that man. This is a time when she would like to mitigate that which might—will—haunt her.

She looks away from him, stands and leaves his room. Double Felix remains where he is and watches where she was; then his hand starts to tremble and he looks at his bar.

My hands are on my knees; my back is straight—an obeisant position I sometimes find useful in seeking self-perspective. Zipper, near me, fills my vision.

I say, "In many ways I feel incapable of living. I feel like I missed class on the day that they told everyone what the big trick is. You know, it's like ripping a phone book in half: no one could ever do it; it sounds impossible; but once you know the technique, it's easy. I can do that. It's a simple little trick, just a way of holding your hands, and you can rip the whole thickness right down the middle. Anyway, I think there's something like that to living, something tiny. Pick up the phone before dialing. Sit in the car before driving. Plug in the computer before programming. Now, I know all the mechanics of living, so tell me: what is the basic first step that eludes me?" As I'm talking, I'm listening to all this. I think I may sound a little too desperate, a little too pathetic.

Biting her lip, presumably assembling a response, Zipper gives it a beat then says, "You can rip a phone book to halves? A real one, like Los Angeles or Las Vegas? Yellow or White?" She bites her lip again, no doubt to hide a smile.

As usual, Zipper has proved herself incapable of disappointing me. What better way for her to respond to my whining, my bemoaning my own bemusement, than to pass it all by and pursue with a puerile delight the possibility of witnessing the Los Angeles Yellow Pages being demonstratively rendered infinitely less accessible than it already is. I can see now that my shortsighted simile will cost Double Felix a phone book.

Okay. After all, who am I to turn even this puny tide. "Wait here," I say. "I'll be right back."

So I go in search of a phone book to rip for Zipper, and as I leave her room and ponder where to begin, I encounter Laurie, blowing out of Double Felix's door and looking none too inclined to conversation. "Hi," I attempt anyway, a careful, approachable, you-can-talk-to-me-cause-I'm-not-a-creep smile pasted on my face. Groaning, she whooshes past me without remark, and I'm left wondering if she's so preoccupied with other matters that she simply didn't see me, or if she's actually annoyed with me personally. Realistically, in light of where she was, I suspect the former, though I'm sure that my vanity would prefer the latter. I think there are some phone books in the kitchen.

The house is pretty quiet—this time in a natural, comforting way—but I can feel the presence of everyone, except of course Timmy. Now that he's gone I cannot begin to imagine where he is, what he is doing.

Swinging past the kitchen door, I see evidence of my earlier visit, untouched and ominously waiting for me; perhaps it would be safer if I learned to clean up after myself. The kitchen, deserted, looks promising as the beginning and end of my quest. It always does. Whenever I'm looking for something I always start here. Rich with myriad cupboards, shelves, pantries, and corners, most of them rarely visited by authorized kitchenfolk bearing authentic kitchenstuff, it is the perfect place to walk into when looking for something. One's heart lightens and one finds oneself confidently musing: Perfect! If it's not here, it's not ANYWHERE!—or at least this one does. Of course, normally it's NOT here but is SOME-WHERE. Today, however, it IS here. The third cupboard I try—at first stubbornly resisting my tug then finally shedding some of its enamel skin—delivers a stack of ancient phone books. I select a Yellow Pages, a good three-incher. *Greater Los Angeles—November 1986*, it proudly announces, sans serif, thus virtually prophesying through its specificity its own imminent obsolescence. In any case it's dusty, has fallen into disuse, is ready for my merciful, index-wrenching blow. I close the cupboard and head home to Zipper, my booty clutched under my arm.

I was right: everyone is here. Maggie is back from whatever she was doing, for I can hear her shower running. I never realized what a penchant that girl has for showers. It brings to mind the phrase well-oiled machine. Maybe she just picked up something on the PCH that needs a good hosing down, in which case I'll have to ignore an extra place for dinner tonight. Double Felix is busy in his room as well, not active, not keeping company, but busily ruminating. This I feel strongly. I can see it well, like a vivid hallucination; I know it as well as if his rubbed-red eyes and sweat-covered neck were sitting before me, cracked lips diffidently hinting that a spot of guidance might be in order. But it won't happen. I won't see it; he won't do it. Not now, and not at quarter after six when I knock on his door. I leave it all behind for the moment. I have a phone book to rip, so I expeditiously pass into Zipper's room, closing the door behind me.

"You found one!" she exclaims upon my return, genuinely looking forward to my performance.

Resuming my seat at her side, I say, "I'm surprised that a woman . . . of great experience . . . such as yourself hasn't seen this before. Surely, dear, it's an old trick. [a frown at this] Not that it's a trick! I mean, I really will rip it down the center. It's just that I would have thought that, over the years, some prurient cathouse bouncer, having assembled a small group for an unauthorized meeting in the linen closet, might have shown this to you and your pals. Or maybe you caught one of the quick acts then showing at your local phone booth on Sunset starring a resourceful junkie, terrified White Pages in hand, quartering for quarters." I like this, and I laugh alone. But I am given to understand by an upraised eyebrow that it's time to move along. "I guess he'd already moved down to the next Sinclair station by the time you got there."

Impatiently: "I never saw it, not anywhere. Now rip it! Rip it and later I'll show you other things that I saw."

This last sounds a bit professional, and though I like that quality in her (it is purely a part of her, a good and real part of her), I dare not comment, for it may upset a balance that we have happily, albeit unwittingly, put into play this afternoon. I can't help but smile at the sparkle in her eyes. I'm not sure, but it seems that women are more capable—or willing—to revert to childhood mannerisms than men, yet they generally carry on in a sublime state of maturity that we can only wonder at; no doubt therein lies the answer.

Positioning the phone book vertically on my lap, I say, "Okay. Here we go."

Zipper giggles, probably at the look of intense concentration fixed on my face. But it is not feigned; it's suddenly very important to me to get this right, to impress my girl with my physical prowess, to not disappoint her, not even in this whim. Most especially not in this whim, for if I'm going to start small—and evidently I am—I should also start well.

CHAPTER EIGHT

"**William, I presume, prompt as usual,** attentive, as always, to the relentless tick-whipping of the clock, as well as to my hourly wishes." This is somewhat muffled, originating, as it is, from behind Double Felix's closed door and in response to my admittedly punctual knock. From where I stand it's six-fifteen.

"No, it's CC," I bellow at the door in my best dude-of-the-streets voice. "I'm lookin' for the methadone clinic. I guess this ain't it, huh?"

Room-crossing sounds, then from just on the other side of the door: "Sorry, CC. You're out of your decade. You're out of style. Try just saying NO."

"NO," I say.

The door swings open. I cross and close it, enter his room as Double Felix walks back to his rumpled but still made-up bed.

Pulling out his desk chair—a forbidden place to sit, though not in so many words—I swing it around and sit facing the bed. My guess is that he'll let this ride, and he does indeed let it pass with merely a halfhearted wince. Childish, yet somehow I enjoy this minor victory. Perhaps it redeems me slightly for being so obediently, so perfectly on time. Perhaps I'm still enamored of myself as William: Ripper of Phone Books. Lying in his bed the way he is, Double Felix looks abject in a way that is very out of character. I can read his frame of mind: better to ignominiously rot on the bed than to face the odium inherent in doing anything else.

"Rough day?" I ask with cocky sarcasm.

Double Felix takes a deep breath, reaches for a nearby glass, and drinks deeply. He is requesting a silence, and I am providing one. Distantly a door slams. From the kitchen there is the sound of something breaking, then being dropped, piece by piece, into a trash can. The cue is thus protracted, self-concluding, unacknowledged.

"William," he says wearily, "my painting is falling asunder. Even now, as we speak—as I speak. And it's my fault. I tried to set it in motion long after it had dried, only to watch in horror as the paint cracks and flakes from the canvas. I have worn out my welcome in the house I made, for my children have grown to resent me."

This seems very much off the track, and I really don't want to sit and listen to more of today's earlier hypernonsense—though the hyper part is seemingly in withdrawal.

"What the fuck are you talking about? I don't understand," I say. "Okay, maybe I see your metaphor, but you've done nothing to bring about the deterioration of things around here. You've been you, just like I've been me." I decide to go ahead and allow something that I think we've both been feeling. "Wake up. Or don't wake up. Either way, you can't accept responsibility for evolution; that won't buy you a way to deny it, and certainly not a way out of it." This came out good, and I'm pleased to see that he's letting it hang for a second. And because I want to tie off the string, I say, "I need a drink. Here, I'll fix yours too."

At his bar I pour the vodka, the gin. This doesn't bother me. Today I learned something from the phone book. I learned that this alcohol is like this bar in Double Felix's room. It's a piece of furniture, an element, not the substance of the foundation, not the motivation behind the blueprint. Not a cause. Not a symptom. Not a result. Not here anyway. Oh yes, I should have been tipped off when I embraced too readily the concept. I dig being an alcoholic. Like these guys who habitually declare bankruptcy, using their cellular phone to make the appointment with their attorney, I get to keep all my rotten eggs in one closeted basket. The party goes on; nothing really changes, just some recondite rules that placate the powers that be through a quick reshuffling of responsibility. Liability is mitigated, interest is assured, principals stand unmolested. Yes . . . (sob) . . . I am an alc . . . an alc . . . an alcoholic (boohoohoohoo). Ultimately, the truest, most cunning, and talented among us boozers recognize what we really have before us, what has fallen so fortuitously in our soggy laps. We get the picture, smile at the familiar fat face reflected amidst the ice cubes, and we behold this declaration, our nifty new tool.

Once, while languishing in a posh Santa Fe hotel with too much money and too little reason to be there, I met and had a short string of successive meals with a rivet broker who serviced the entire Southwest eleven months out of the year while keeping his wife and kids facial-ed and fed in Phoenix. Like myself, he was in a hurry to spend a lot of money without acquiring the burden of something to show for it; that is, ephemerally. This proved a bit more difficult than it should have been, as I was enjoying my torpor and so was confining my sexual gratification to glossy magazines and a balcony that overlooked a high school abundantly endowed with fine girls stuffed with the stuff of which future legends are to be made; in short, I was happy with myself. My acquaintance—Dennis, it was—Dennis was growing antsy, a mite fearful, I conjectured then, of spending so much time in the company of another man . . . over meals . . . at a hotel: he was definitely worried about one of us. So one night at the hotel bar, he said to me,

"Bill, listen. I know a great cathouse down in Albuquerque. The girls are fucking gorgeous. It costs a fucking fortune, but it's worth it! Okay, it's not worth it, but it's closer than home. [much laughter here] Who cares? My treat. Whaddaya say? Let's have another drink and drive down there in my Lincoln. It'll be a blast. C'mon, I'm fucking horny, and I don't want to wake up next to you tomorrow morning." (nervous laughter here) I turned to my drink, reluctantly shaking my head over it, and whined, "Aw, I don't know, Dennis. I hate the smell of those places. I hate the smell of the baby powder—you know how they all smell like baby powder? Well, I hate that." I looked up smiling affably: What's the next plan? I sure would like to hear it! But he looked dubious, so I continued. "See, I'm allergic to that stuff. The last time a girl put that stuff on me, I broke out in a rash." I looked up solemnly: that's right, a rash! Then went on: "So you see, I don't think it's such a good idea." But he was unimpressed. "Fuck that," he bellowed. "Tell 'em to use oil!" I shook my head again, "Well, yeah . . . But see, just the smell is enough to make me sick, and you know all those places smell like that damn powder." Dennis could see he had lost. He hung his head. I did too, realizing, for the first time, that he was afraid to go alone. "Fuck," he muttered. "I never saw anyone not go to a cathouse cause of baby-fucking-powder." He drained his drink. We had eaten our last meal together.

Later, alone in my room, I remembered that I really was allergic to baby powder. This fact so amused me that I almost called his room to report it: Hey Dennis, guess what? Turns out I wasn't lying after all! I really am allergic to baby powder! Instead I tried to jerk off while thinking about Dennis—sort of a malicious act—but it was a no-go.

As I hand him his drink and sit again in his desk chair, Double Felix says, "I am so frustrated and disillusioned with the petty feelings of others, so confounded by the way they misinterpret what I am about."

"What are you about?" I ask, not at all expecting an answer.

He takes a drink and pushes his finger through his dirty (for the first time since I have known him) hair, and says somewhat regretfully, "If you could only understand—really see—how I've painted my life, then, William, you would know me for an artist. Every action is a brushstroke. No detail is ever too small for consideration or revision. I do everything, and that which is beyond my control, that which just happens, is tire-lessly scrutinized and evaluated. So you see, it is all just as I would have it. I am responsible for . . . I am responsible."

Stuff of old, the makings of a mythical Morning Vodka. But not really, for far from being merely a cool observation, this is about him . . . now . . . with no margin for error. Oh so different from our discussion just hours ago or the discussion just hours before that. This is new ground. One will be hard-pressed to find a chortle in these proceedings, for here we shall be digging deep in our pockets for change to feed the meter. The red flag is imminent. The maid is watching. A folded bill wrapped in a witticism and rendered with a wink won't work here. That ain't the way to grease palms in this county.

"I see that," I say. "I really do, but what good does that do? What is there in my sanction of your art that can help you to move forward—or to not move forward—contentedly?"

Seeing him up close, touching his pain and wanting to assuage it, I suddenly feel woefully inadequate for the task at hand. But from this I glean a sense of universality, perhaps even abstract fellowship, and I am certain that no man true of heart could call himself a healer of his brother's broken spirit. One does what one can; therein lie the minutes that comprise a finest hour.

Tears well in his eyes, and he looks at me as if to make sure that I see this weakness. He appears both frustrated that I need to have him spell it out, and relieved that he finally has an opportunity to do just that.

"No one can be this alone for this long," he sobs. "I have done wrong—so very long ago—and I built a world of contrivance on that foundation. Then you came, and I embraced you for reasons that I didn't then understand. I used you, but I loved you too. For a long time it seemed to me that you had no role to play here; now I know why you're here." Lifting his left arm with what seems to be an unnatural effort, he makes a crippled sweeping gesture to indicate our surroundings. "William, I need you to tell me that this—all of this—is okay. What I've done. Me. Is it all okay with you?"

Overwhelming, a bit, all of this is, and though I understand but little of these particulars, I feel that I see well the whole, and I am comfortable in rendering an answer. "It always has been; however, I do not know if it will remain so."

Double Felix nods. "Understood," he says. "In time I shall produce the means by which you may make the latter determination."

He sets about drying his eyes in an odd fashion, almost striking himself with dual fists, rotating them briefly against his face as would a child. I look away, preferring to fix my sights on the tower of ice in my glass. And for now things get quiet as I look at my glass. I'm in a vacuum that seems to be growing impatient with the plenum of my flesh; naturally, I too feel abhorred.

An ice cube collapses and drops lower to meet its limpid fate. The sound startles me, and I am surprised to find that some time has passed, for my ice has all but melted. I am left with a drink that is weaker, albeit more voluminous. Such is the state of things in my glass. Perhaps it is time to leave.

I throw my head back and narrow my eyes—an impulsive and hopeless attempt to appear guileful, but why?—and prepare to announce my retreat to the big room, though in truth I have no idea where I'll go. But I am derailed by the sight of Double Felix smiling, almost mirthfully, at me. Surprise! This is not the mien of a man who, moments before, was pounding his head in tearful self-abasement; in any case, it's not at all what I expected to see.

"Gee, Double Felix, you're looking better already," I manage. "Glad to have been of help." Completing the act, I look at my wrist and say, "Well, gotta shove off! Don't hesitate to call if there's ever anything else I can do for you." I begin to rise but immediately give up and settle back in my chair. Habit. Fate. I know he has something to say, and I know that I must hear it.

I allow the waves their piece of the conversation, until I can stand it no more and ask, "Why are you smiling? I thought we just established that you're miserable, woeful, and wretched. I can understand a bit of levity to raise your spirits, but you look positively fucking blithe." Then, in widely measured syllables, half mocking my own irritation: "What Fuck-Ing Gives?"

He blows me a kiss and says, "It's just women, right? I mean, provided that we maintain this, the correct perspective, we should be safe. After all, what can they do that we can't handle? What havoc might they wreak which we may not quell? What bitchery could any of them possibly bestow on us that we could not cast aside with a mere drunken pinch? A goose and a pat? Who exactly among them can we not physically dispatch? Who among them can we not facilely dispense with?" And he folds his arms over his chest as if to underscore the self-evidence of this spurious resolution.

I should have guessed—I almost did. True to form, Double Felix seeks refuge behind sarcasm. So I missed it: it is a joke. I look at him, intending to accuse him of trying to be clever. But I see in his smirk that he is trying to be clever, so I say nothing and feel better—better than both of us. This room and this man are less well known to me than they were only hours ago, or I to them. Something long latent is no longer; it is in our faces. I can leave this room now, take my glass of gin and only partially interrupt the conversation. Like a film parody of a man stepping outside of himself, becoming translucent as a function of his duplicity, part of me would remain, and to whatever end it would bring him, it would be the part that Double Felix values most.

For I now see that I am a permanent part of this world that Double Felix finds so central to his endurance. Long ago he plotted an equation that holds values for length-of-stay and impact-of-stay. I've located enough points with him over a long enough period of time to know that I fall on that line, will always be on that line, run with that line. Given that a line, by definition, is of infinite length, my presence is assured indefinitely—whether I'm here or not. Laurie, having accumulated virtually no length-of-stay coordinates, arrived with copious impact-of-stay points already laid down, and so runs as well on that line—and did before she even showed up. We are proved, she and I.

"William, before you go could you fill my glass?" he asks, though I haven't mentioned leaving. "I would, of course, do it myself, but—this I admit only to you—I feel that my previous hour of grief led me to a hint of overindulgence, and walking may be more than I can manage for the next hour or so."

I fetch his glass. He flashes a surprisingly charming—considering the context—smile. He is indeed committed to detail.

"Oh . . . and one more thing," he continues. "Could you find that stainless steel pan in the bathroom—you know, the one I used to use?"

Indeed I do know the pan to which he refers; I had all but forgotten it. Shortly after Double Felix and I began sharing Morning Vodka, he fell victim to a strange and protracted stomach disorder. Without warning, over a period of about six weeks, he was subject to sudden attacks of intense nausea, often followed—naturally—by violent vomiting. Characteristically unwilling to consult a doctor over so vague and sporadic an ailment, he settled instead on a large stainless steel pan, selected and permanently removed from kitchen duty, which he kept by his side at all times. Sure enough, just as he predicted, his little puking problem—he called it that—faded away, into obscurity like just another short-term and unpleasant guest. The pan, lid and all, got polished one afternoon by the puker himself and stowed away in his bathroom, presumably for quick access in the event of a relapse.

I have no trouble locating it in his impeccably spotless bathroom: without a doubt the only bathroom on god's green where stainless steel cookware is present in greater quantities than stray hairs or wadded-up Kleenexes. I swing by his bar. No point in mentioning the likely cross-purposes of the two; I simply deliver the pan and the vodka to his bedside. While not asleep, he looks as though he might be momentarily.

"Thank you, William," he says in a low voice.

Without speaking, without knowing why, I place my palm on his forehead and push back his wayward hair—an odd and maternal gesture that draws no visible acknowledgment—and I step gently from his room.

What follows I do not witness, for I am well along the hallway, but moments after I leave his room, closing his door behind me, Double Felix swings abruptly out of his bed—not so much in response to my departure, but more as if he has just remembered some forgotten appointment—and tiptoes over to his desk. Here he opens one of the smaller drawers and extracts a strip of three photographs—the type produced by a coin-operated photo booth.

Not looking at, but returning to his bed with the strip, he settles back against his pillows. Only when he is still does he hold away and examine the photographs. One image, thrice repeated with only subtle variations, it is himself, looking only superficially younger, and Laurie, looking profoundly younger; in fact, she is a mere girl.

He sees the two faces, but they do not bring to him that which he is seeking. They are too small, too flat, too inexorably motionless. He reaches for his drink, and as his hand falls from his lap he catches sight of the shiny pan lid on the floor at his side. He reaches down and picks it up.

Double Felix breathes condensation onto the convex surface and wipes over it a shine once felt and now lifted from his bedding, the bedding of another house, the bedding of erections, the bedding of Laurie. His face swells in distortion with the curvature of the improvised mirror as he mimics his own expression, captured some years earlier in that curtained photo booth with Laurie seated tidily on his lap. The photo strip is held up next to his cheek. His eyes move randomly among the seven faces, each misshapen by the arc of its reflection.

CHAPTER NINE

The hall sucks me along its ineluctable path: a great big wet throat with a world of guilt waiting at the end, the rooms like so many teeth surrounding me. The women that occupy these rooms cry out for recognition in a collective voice louder than any heard before here, during those fresher and more playful times of this house's intention. Most vociferous is Laurie, and . . . Maggie. Please, of all people, don't let it be her. Not that I really give a rat's ass what happens to the fucker. Just let me get the fuck out of here without knowing about it. I don't want to know any of it. I don't want to see any of it. But the last thing I need is Maggie . . . more makeup—just a touch—and that should just about fucking do it. YessssssOkay. There. Done.

Fuck this! I put down my fucking liner, and six things fall off my fucking vanity.

God but this place is a fucking mess. I need to talk to Double Felix about that maid—cleaning woman—whatever! Why she can't find two extra seconds in her dreary little life to keep my vanity clean is beyond me. I mean PLEASE! Fuck me! What the hell did I do to become a second-class citizen around here? Sometimes I think I should just walk. And won't they be just a little surprised then. I'd just like to get one good look at their faces when they try to have a party without Maggie and her friends around. Wouldn't be so crowded around here then, would it? Fat fucking chance! Oh, I can see it now: music, food for a hundred, and nobody here to eat it, just William and Double Felix sitting drunk in a corner, fighting over Laurie's tricycle seat.

Maybe a tad more shadow. I can't fucking find it! I just had it . . . Oh, there. I pick it up, but no, I don't need it.

Sometimes I wonder what I've accomplished here in the last six months. Sometimes I wonder why I'm not catching. It's ME waiting here! I'm pretty. I'm in Los Angeles. I know people. I fuck, for chrissake—I fuck a lot! What else can I do? Do I have to sit at this godforsaken bus stop forever? This is your room, Maggie. Help yourself to the bar, Maggie. Feel free to invite people over, Maggie. You're welcome to stay as long as you like, Maggie. Let me know if you ever need a little extra pocket money, Maggie. Great, but what's in it for ME? What's really in it for me? How come a cheap little kid like Laurie can walk in here and turn the place upside down? Laurie's here and all of a sudden nobody could care less about Maggie. Even William, who's wanted to fuck me since he first saw me at that party, is so preoccupied with the silly bitch that he messed up his one and only opportunity—I mean, c'mon: I know the guy's a stiff, but he must do better than that when he's with his little whore; those girls don't stick around for the scenery.

So anyway, I think I'll just—it must be well past six by now. I think I'll just drift out to the big room—hell with this fucking hole; I feel like a woodpecker . . . no, chucker . . . oh whatever. I think I'll just go right ahead and drift on out to the big room and see what's what.

What's what in me, in my room. It may not be my house, but it should be. Just who's gonna tell me what I do and don't deserve? Just because—okay, maybe I can't put my finger on it. Fine, maybe I haven't the slightest fucking clue what it is. But there for sure is something special in me. There IS. I know there is, because if there wasn't I would just die, and I can't die; I'm not even anywhere close to wanting to die. No way. No, I want to live. I'm living now; I was living yesterday—way before I came to this place; that was only six months ago, about six months ago, and I'll be living tomorrow. THAT'S how I know there's something special in me. I don't have to know what or where. I just think about it, and there I am.

So I guess I'll just drift out to the big room and see what's what out there. I open my door—but wait: I can hear someone's coming, so I pull back and wait till they pass, then stick my head out.

It's Laurie! and she has her little bag of stuff with her! So I bet she's leaving, and because I can't resist—and dying to know what's what—I step on out, just drifting like I was anyway, to the big room.

"Laurie," I tell her, "where are you off to? What's that you've got? Fuck, that's not your stuff, is it? I hope you're not leaving us already. Probably just going off for the night, right? Probably see you in the morning. Well, you just go right ahead and have a good time. Sorry to bother you." She's just standing there looking at me with her wise-ass eyes. She's waiting for me to finish. Almost. "And if you want to talk when you get home, about anything, anything at all, or if you're just feeling low, well, you just come and knock on Maggie's door, and we'll have ourselves a nice talk. Toodle-loo," I tell her.

"Why are you here, Maggie?" she says to me, and that bitch says it none too nicely to boot.

This is so perfect that she should ask me this. Typical of these know-nothing little cunts who suddenly realize, right in the middle of their worthless little lives, that they have an upper hand over fools like Double Felix or William, or any other fool—and they are all fools. Of course, I'm stuck with what I've got, going along playing it straight when a half-ass coquette tramp like Laurie is so incapable of handling what she's got—and god only knows why she got it—that she only manages to bounce around making trouble everywhere and doing nothing for herself. What am I doing here? I'm here because I know what I'm doing! That's what I'm doing here. So—and not that she would ever see this—the real question is: what is she doing here?

So we stare at each other awhile, and not that I feel compelled or anything, but because I'm staying and she's not, I tell her, "I belong here."

Here she gets this obnoxious little look on her face like she wants to be friendly all of a sudden, like it's fucking sisterhood night here in the hallway, like she suddenly has some sort of understanding that I don't have. Of course this is the typical reaction of a cornered brat, not to mention the typical reaction of someone who's about to bail out. They always want to get mushy when it's splitsville.

"I know you do, Maggie," she says. "Goodbye."

And she turns and walks out of the hall and through the big room. I hear the front door close behind her. I know you do, Maggie. What nerve!

So I wait till she's gone, and I go and sit on the couch in the big room. Of course the remote for the TV is nowhere to be found, and there's absolutely nothing happening in here. Nothing. I wish I had a place to bail out of—a real place. At least Laurie got to have me watch her leave, and, of course, Double Felix and William will be broken-hearted puppies for the next few days, until either another tramp lands in their sequential beds or they can drink her out of their sequential heads. If only she knew how fast she'll be forgotten. She probably thinks she did all kinds of permanent heart carving around here: What a joke! She'll be lost in the fog of their morning drinks before she can find a seat on the next dick. But at least she gets some temporary notice.

Fuck, if I walked out of here right now no one would miss me till they needed something. A party. A hand job in the shower at four in the morning: here's my rent, Mr. Double Felix. Squirt, squirt. Not really: a secret. Double Felix and the endless hand job. Nothing hard about it, just a secret among us girls who like to have pussies licked and nothing more.

Speak of the devil: I think I hear his door opening. Yes, there's that crisp step—well, a little soggy, but at least now I'll have some company. Oh, to be so lucky. Dare I think that Mr. Double Felix will want to talk with me, with just Maggie? Of course not! He's looking for Laurie. Ooooh! I wonder if I should say anything? I mean, well, I guess I have to—fuck, I can never seem to sit straight on this fucking couch—though I hate to be the one. But it won't be so bad, maybe the best way to get a little attention. Unless he knows. Maybe he kicked her out. Yeah, fat fucking chance of that. So he's definitely coming down the hall. Okay. So, what the fuck am I supposed to do? I mean, he's stuck with me, right? If he asks, I'll tell him. If it comes up, it comes up. After all, I'm not the fucking social—I really need some new clothes—director around here. Maybe I should try, really try this time, to bring him off. It has been awhile, but who knows what he wants, and the booze doesn't help matters. Maybe I should take a different room. Maybe there's something he could do for me that we haven't thought of. I really should try to talk to him more often—not like I don't make myself available enough as it is. I wish that fucking remote was around. Too late. But maybe I should be watching TV.

Here he is, and he says, "Maggie. What a delightful find you are. It just seems like ages since we've spent time together, doesn't it?"

I can tell right off that he's really fucked up, but what else is new? It's only par for the fucking course, so I let him go on.

"Maggie, you haven't seen Laurie around, have you? I was hoping to have a word with her." So here we go. He looks at me like my dog used to whenever I opened a can of food: hungry and hopeful.

Okay. No big deal. Let's get it over with. I tell him, "To tell you the truth, I don't know for sure what's what with her; she and I didn't talk much."

He really is drunk. He looks positively vapid. But this is kind of fun, in a way.

I give him a second to digest what I said, then I tell him, "But, since my first loyalty is to you, I think I should tell you that I did see her walk out of here a few minutes ago, and she had what looked like her stuff . . . you know, her little bag."

He doesn't say anything. It's kinda weird and uncomfortable, and I'm starting to wonder if he even heard me. Then, as if he was taking time just to work up his next move, he smiles politely, like he does when he's drunk at a party, and walks to the front door. But he stops without even putting his hand on the knob. He bangs his head once against the door, and I'm glad that he's turned away from me because I'm embarrassed. After all, I'm not the fucking camp counselor around here. I don't know what to say, but I really can't just leave.

"Can I make you a drink, Double Felix?" I say.

"Sure, thanks," he says. He sounds okay, but his back is still to me. He sounds like he's trying to get a grip, which is fucking-fine-o with me.

From the bar I tell him, "You shouldn't take it so hard. Laurie . . . well, Laurie is a nice girl and all, but I just don't see her as really being cut out for our . . . for our little family." Eeeek! Saying that makes me want to gag, but I couldn't think of anything else. "And you know what? I don't think she was very happy here anyway. I think she sort of sensed that she didn't quite fit in." No response from him to this. "I hope she realized that she could have come to me. Hell, I know how much you liked her, and I would have done anything to make her feel at home. If only she would have said something." Still nothing. I don't even think the fucker is listening to me.

But I must have said something right, because when he finally does turn around he's wearing a fucking ear-to-ear grin. He says, "No, it's fine, Maggie. Let her go; what do we care? Why, indeed, should you and I care about a girl like that? She doesn't understand people like us, does she?"

So I don't know what's what with this drinking ritual that Double Felix and William go through every day; but whatever it is to them, Double Felix looks like he could sure use it right now. I've never seen him look like this before: kind of twitchy, kind of leering. It's almost spooky. He's always so damn aloof, but now he seems downright lecherous. It sort of makes me wish I never fucked him. I finish making his drink, but instead of taking it over to him like I was planning to do, I just leave it on the bar and go back to the couch.

"I hope that's okay," I tell him with one of those smiles I used to use as a kid. I worked in the coat-check room at a restaurant after school. I used to wear this black bra, and you could see it through my white blouse. Wooden hanger, sir? And that was a fucking dollar right there.

I think my voice sounds too formal. I hope he doesn't notice.

He doesn't move for his drink. His eyes just follow me from where he is, and he says, "Does she, Maggie? She doesn't understand people like us, does she?"

I guess he's not about to give this up, so I tell him, "No, she doesn't. I'm sure you'll find somebody much more interesting to take her place." Oh, this is good. This is a good other subject. I don't like the way this Laurie talk is going. "And Timmy's gone too. You have to replace him.

And we already had that empty room to start with. That's three rooms you have to fill! That's why it's getting so fucking boring around here—not that it's boring. I mean, fuck, now that I think about it, I'm out here alone with William and Zipper. And believe me," I tell him, confidential-like because I've always suspected that those two are taking advantage of him, "those love birds don't make a lot of room for anyone else. I might as well be alone."

"Oh, you're not alone, Maggie, definitely not alone," he says while moving away from the door. He still looks strange, and it's starting to bother me, and I hope he gets back to normal soon. Then, like it's the only place to sit, he comes to the couch and sits next to me. I make like I'm trying to adjust my underwear, but it's all I can do to look casual as I move down to the corner.

"No, no, I know I'm not," I tell him. "I just thought it would do us all some good to see some new faces around here."

He moves next to me. I suppose if he wants to fuck I could just go along; I mean, it's not like it would be anything new or anything. But he just seems real creepy right now, like there's something wrong, and I'm not sure I could do it.

"I've been thinking about you incessantly," he says—he's right up against me, but I've got to hear this. "I've been pondering what we are to each other, as well as what we could be." Knowing that I'm listening now, he reclines slightly away from me. "You and I, Maggie, we have some invisible threads tying us together—I'm sure you're aware of this—and I think it's time we fostered those connections. I think, Maggie, that it's time we thought about your future."

His hand is on my thigh—inside my thigh. It's just there, like it might be on his own thigh. I feel very confused, and I really don't know what to think or do. This is so fucked, but I even wish—no, I exactly wish—that Zipper were here with me. I don't know why, but somehow it all feels wrong. Yet I have to listen; this might be important. So I'm still.

I say, "What about it?"

His eyes jump, sort of wild. "It's with me, just me. Away from here. In another place, maybe another country, anywhere you want. We'll have our own house. You can have your own room if you want, and all the things you want and all the friends you want!"

"I don't understand. Why? I mean, we have all that now, don't we?"

He stops dead for a second, then his head starts shaking real fast. Finally he finds his tongue. "No, no. No, no, no! Different from this! Don't you see, I'm talking about our place—like a family." His hand is almost on my pussy now, but believe it or not, I don't think he knows it.

"I still don't get it. Do you mean . . . like married?" I don't know if I should be saying this, but I don't know what else to say.

His mouth falls open. He looks a little crushed, or more like he never thought I would say that. Oh, I hope I didn't make him too mad. Damn! I better fuck him now. I'd just better fuck him. I'd better just lie back and let him go down for as long as he wants. I don't have the slightest clue what this is all about, so I should just fuck him. That must be it. He's all fucked up, and he's not himself, and that's what this is leading to.

I tell him, "Look, I didn't mean that. I'm just confused—you know, sort of depressed about Laurie, just like you are." I try putting my hand on his hand. "I know what: let's forget about all this and give our minds a rest. How about it? You know, I haven't seen your room for ages. Why don't we go in there and have a drink or something?"

But I can't figure out what's what, because his eyes narrow and he says in a very serious voice, like he really wants to know all of a sudden, "How old are you, Maggie?"

What a fucking weird question. I pull back a little, but still his hand doesn't move. He must be really fucked up, or getting paranoid, or something. I laugh like it's a silly question—and it is. "Why," I tell him, "did you spot some vice cops in the hallway? Old enough, if that's what you're worried about. Anyway, it's a little late to be screening me, wouldn't you say?"

"Nothing like that. I know you're old enough, Maggie."

Fucker! Fucker! I can't believe this! My face is getting hot. Fuck! I just know the fucker's going to see me blush. I can't get upset. I can't get upset. I've got to get to my room.

"What the hell does that mean?" I ask him. I can't let my voice crack.

His hand's right on me now. "Nevermind," he says. "You're right. I do need another drink. We need another drink. Let's go to my room."

He's smiling now. He's trying to be himself, and I don't care, and I can feel my fucking eyes tearing up—right here in front of him. I've got to get to my room!

Turning off to the side—the other. No, I put my head down—wait. I scratch my eyes. I rub my eyes. "I've got my period, Double Felix. I've got to go to my room now."

I try to get up, but he holds me. By my pussy! He's holding me down by pressing on my fucking pussy!

He says, "No you don't, Maggie. You don't get your period for another week."

But as soon as he says it he slumps away. He just sort of collapses into a little ball on the couch. I don't know if he's passed out. I don't know how he could know that. I don't know how he could say that. I just have to go. I just have to go to my room. I almost knock over the fucking table on my way to the hall, and then I bang into a chair. I think I skinned my knee. I think Double Felix saw it.

CHAPTER TEN

... **Maggie has been rendered comparatively silent** because of it, almost inversely so, a condition that somehow makes her even more conspicuous.

Beckoning, the deck awaits at the end of the hall, the end of this day. The inside of this house has grown too volatile, as well it should, being an adept mimic of the inside of Double Felix's room, a sort of parallel universe. I can hear Maggie playing with her makeup, threatening to bump into me as I pass her door, and I don't want that to happen. I need my deck and my thoughts, need the time to drink and settle into my chaise before sunset, for I intend to be in place with time to spare. I need this sunset. I need some sort of punctuation.

Almost home—the end of the hall and I swing through a wide single double door, springing, more or less, directly to the bar where I resolutely pour myself the stiffest of gins so that I might irresolutely pass out at evening's end. I shall consider Double Felix and his house. I shall wonder after myself.

My chaise is cold; either it has missed my warming weight or it is anticipating the inevitable night. I mount it with mixed feelings and suffer the usual moments of reintroduction. It seems always to give readily at first, adapting to my difficult shape, but as I sleep it will retake its ground, and I will awaken in the middle of the night with a skeleton that has been coerced into compatibility with a piece of patio furniture. Though this is, perhaps, a small price to pay for cogent reassertion of my general indoor/outdoor character. Oh yes! My restless spirit has led me back to the sea—or sight of same—for I acknowledge no bounds within the property lines of Double Felix's not-so-real estate.

How unreal it now seems to think back on streets, stretches of sidewalk, or vast parking lots, garages, levels down, levels up. Difficult to imagine the reckless intrepidity that must have surged through my veins as I seized the day, steering wheel in hand, in a sovereign state, under no condition, bound and well determined to witness parts un-or-little-known, it is difficult indeed.

"Dif-fi-cult," I say protractedly and to my feet. But soft, for it was not difficult. No, it was the easiest thing in the world.

Why then have I lost myself? What then is the device of my self-incarceration? And if such a thing is possible, how then have I sullied my life?

A girl comes to mind, young, perhaps fifteen. I knew her slightly—actually I knew of her—and she was not unlike Zipper in certain ways, though my experience with her is in no manner analogous to my relationship with Zipper.

I was buried in the middle years of high school, very much an introvert and rather disrespectful of popular trends. Such an attitude made me a constant target of abuse by those whose main objective is to impress their fellow abusers. In short, I was not liked and was somewhat disenchanted with the society of my fellows. The girl—her name was Patty—was quite attractive and predictably in with the in-crowd, as it were. Cornered by her at my locker one afternoon, I turned crimson, became sweaty and unsteady, adrenaline flowing in abject dread of the psychological assault I was about to face. To the delight of her growing audience, she came very close to me in a mock seduction. She reached for my hand and tried to place it on her breast; failing in that, she rubbed her breast on my arm. She played with my hair, reached for my crotch, licked my cheek, all accompanied by a salacious, albeit loud, whisper of concepts which theretofore had been most abstract to me. Finally, with me on the verge of obvious trauma and the crowd quite engaged, she delivered the *coup de grace*. Swiftly and shamelessly she thrust her hand into her own jeans and did . . . what? All I knew is that just as swiftly her finger—presumably pungent, though I was in no way attentive to this sort of detail—was ignobly proffered to me, specifically under my nose, thrust clumsily, deflected from my lip, leaving what may have been a wet spot on already sweaty turf. The onlookers roared with laughter. I was shamed to the point of panic and swung wildly with my arms, catching her, I believe, in the face with a textbook and breaking through the semicircle of my tormentors in a maniacal run.

I spent the next two weeks at home, cloistered in my room while my mother, ignorant of what had happened, did her best to field irate phone calls from Patty's father who was demanding her firstborn in exchange for the bruise on his daughter's cheek. "What happened?" my mother asked me, knowing me too well to believe PattyDad's claim that I had maliciously attacked his daughter. I was ostensibly down with a bug, though this was really just for the benefit of my father, for unlike my mother, he was not entirely sensitive to the hell that was my high school. "Nothing, Mom," I said from my pillow. "It was an accident. I turned around too fast and my book hit her." And though my mother understood that I hadn't told her the whole truth, she also knew, as did I, that what I told her was true.

The days spent in my room during those two weeks were surprisingly rich with growth, or at least I came to terms with many things (maybe as good a definition of growth as any). I saw that I was in my room because I had betaken myself there, not because of Patty or her actions. I saw that Patty herself was as much a victim as I was, and because her injury stemmed from her own weakness—a weakness I didn't suffer from—I felt silently and privately vindicated. And, most amazingly, I felt that Patty, had she the means to comprehend the hurt she would cause me, would not have done what she did. I came out of that room and went back into hell with a faith in the basic goodness of Patty and company, and thanks to a stubborn disregard of any evidence to the contrary, I am certain that it was this belief that carried me safely into adulthood.

But now I find myself in a different room, a big and airy room replete with women, wishes, and water. If there's a way out of this room, if there's a way off of this deck, then it lies in the revelation of a basic goodness that lies a great deal closer to home than Patty or her friends, or, for that matter, closer than Maggie, Timmy, Double Felix, even closer than Zipper.

These are and always shall be merely my problems. Even at their most dreadful and tenacious, I have always viewed the conditions of my life as in hand, things to be attended to in due time. Whether or not I effect any changes, whether or not I ever seriously give it thought, whether or not I really gaze into the mirror, is all small potatoes to me. For it's only me, only my life, and there's nothing so awful that I can't simply absorb it into my general condition. These matters of my self-esteem are perhaps trivial; I find a more seemly diversion in Double Felix, for I sense that his escape from this house must be necessarily more tempestuous than mine.

There emanates from the big room a kind of vacuum of perception— but this is not exactly what I mean; call it a blind search. It is there always; it is there in strength now. I smell desperation from that room. It blends with the general odor of the house that is encroaching—has encroached—on my deck. The erstwhile pure and robust air of the Pacific already far too overwhelmed by its own impending extinction to afford much assistance, the smell hangs about pervasively, like a pimp, or a friendly debt. There are doings in the big room, doings of Double Felix and doings of Maggie. Their nature is likely a matter of record, for they have been bespoken as I mused and are currently winding down. I don't wish to consider them; they are more meaningfully addressed in the general.

I suspect that Double Felix is a man of great attachments, and that these attachments play a pivotal role in his life. More than simple infatuations with people—that would be the outward appearance—Double Felix is addicted to systems, maybe to one very elemental system. I wonder to what lengths a man will go, or fail to go, to construct that world in which he hopes to find his truest happiness.

Such a man might be an aging athlete. Secretly ashamed of his reputation, feeling the need to validate it on a daily basis, he ultimately tarnishes it by insistently riding his downward curve. A gaze is averted, and the popular talk turns respectfully to his prime, though the athlete senses only condescension. Such a man might be a convict, more specifically, an ex-convict. A virtual lifetime of learning and society spent in the recondite world of prison, he is suddenly dropped into the world at large. Disorientation aside, this man has dreamt and longed for a world that the rest of us know simply does not exist. Even if it did, what reality can compete with a fantasy? What woman doesn't improve with an airbrush, gloss, and staples? The convict longs now not for a wife, kids, and house, but rather for guards, prison card games, and a tight-assed plenum of microcosmic government. He makes old contacts, kindles old impulses. If he possesses even a modicum of wisdom he knows precisely what he is doing. Or such a man might be a woman, might in fact be a mother. Viewed externally, she is a former mother, for her children no longer require her. But that's a minor detail and has no bearing on what she is inside of herself. She knows things that I will never know. Her biological imperative is long asleep; this she thinks about every day. But no matter: there are grandchildren to babysit, in the morning a Scout troop to make cookies and lemonade for.

I wonder if Double Felix has any children. He somehow chimes the notes of a sire, perhaps one caught in an aberrant opus; a monarch cursed with too many X chromosomes; a praying mantis who, failing to get his head bitten off, has outlived his purpose; a disgraced father whose proclivities reside outside the acceptable, or even the right. Maybe Double Felix has no children—I really can't imagine that he would—and maybe therein lies much of the timber of his construction. I shall have to remember never to ask him.

It is a cool evening, cooler than the last. The sun plays one of its best tricks, accelerating, plunging faster and faster into the horizon. But as it is with the surprising largeness of a low moon, this is merely our mistake, for this speed and that size are for our purposes constant; our perception of them changes as they near our terra-turfa, our best-loved reference point.

Our lives are short to the degree that we're all basically stuck with— at best—this huge spherical prison; there will be no other quarters. Best of the only possible world, digs this big are far too big. Spiraling inward, we frantically seek to diminish our domains, to seek out more effective agents of our confinements. We're terrified of overexposure to the enormous scope of experience out there. It makes us tiny, and we don't want to be tiny. We want to be big fish in well-kept aquariums. Long ago I grew attached to Los Angeles and was loath to leave even for a short trip. Now I confine my travels to the wrought construct of this house. Even that has become a bit much; witness my attachment to the deck. I sleep out here now—a month from now will I live out here? By then Double Felix will have likewise confined himself to his room, and we will be hard pressed to continue Morning Vodka. Thus we will have assisted each other that much further in our respective internal quests. Will I take the logical last step and drink myself to an eternal frozen sleep in this very chaise, to be found the next day by Double Felix's latest luv interest? Reduced to watching her masturbate, he will have sent her out to me to deliver a lukewarm glass of vodka and a hoary witticism. Later she might ask him, "Is your friend always blue and hard like that? I was just wondering." Double Felix will mourn me as he nods off. He'll dream about Zipper, wisely departed for parts unknown, and me. He'll dream that we all loved each other in ways that we could understand.

The sun is getting ready to test the water. To my rear and left, from a small and rarely accessed utility shed that sits behind the kitchen, I hear sounds. Someone is rooting about in there, but the efforts sound slow and deliberate, not the hurried rummaging of a burglar or any other potential security threat. Probably Maggie, who once sought a volleyball in that very shed, has returned there in search of some other obnoxious outdoor recreational apparatus. I am too lazy and destined to spectate. Though I should seize this aurally procured advantage over the others and set about warming up for a raucous game of tetherball, I choose instead to rise to another drink and set about warming up for a cold and quiet night. With difficulty I stand, lift the bottle from the bar, and repair with it back to my chaise.

Arriving late—I just now hear it, but it has the insistent aspect of something repeated or soundly completed—a noise in the form of an unpracticed sniffle reaches me, settled but a moment in my synthetic cradle. Maggie then makes herself further known to me with a cough, and I am compelled to turn about.

"Come here," I say without forethought, with some urgency, as a pure reaction to her obvious distress.

She is clearly upset and in need of companionship. Unexpected, but I can only surmise that she came here to find me, and I of course will rise to the occasion, though I do find it somewhat unsettling to behold a woman in want of solace from me; better were it again Double Felix, with whom I share some common weakness.

She willingly shuffles over to me and fills my proffered palms with her trembling hands. "I didn't know who else to talk to," she says.

"What about Laurie?" I say. Admittedly callous, this is, not to mention improbable, but her appeal has caught me off guard, and in lieu of an actual response, I manage merely to address the superficial and immediate sense of her statement. I'm torn between wanting to know what it is that got to her and why it is she came to me with it.

She pulls back and recovers nicely, accepting my impropriety lightly with a glimmer of what I know to be Maggie. "Laurie left for good. I saw her. Anyway, William, I'm sure you figured out that she and I never really hit it off," she says, but her eyes say: Okay? Can we move on now?

Grasping enough of a handle to know that it's not time to prod her about Laurie, I swallow this silently and deliver to her hands a gentle, genuine squeeze. "I'm sorry; never mind that. Tell me what."

She stands away and gains a chair behind her. She does this without looking first to locate the chair, and this small adroitness is quietly respectable to me: that, despite her obvious disconcertion, upon entering the deck she reflexively noted the location of this chair and listed it accordingly as a possible player in one of many possible moves, any of which would serve to strengthen my perception of her physical grace. It's as if the arrogance of her body was enhanced to compensate for the temporary absence of arrogance from her attitude; a chaser to assist in the pride-swallowing.

"Things aren't what they used to be," she tells me, seasoning it with the reluctance offered an inquisitive child by a parent whose duty it is to reveal yet another aspect of the world's ugliness to a hopeful and virginal mind. "I don't think . . . I don't think I'm the sort of person who can deal with it . . . or even understand it."

This latter, spoken as a confession, touches me not only because it was hard for her to say, but also because I had no idea that Maggie was so frail. I wince inwardly, invisibly. I'm the one who's supposed to be frail and weak around here, not the women. I need strength from the women, and direction; all of them, even Maggie. *What are you saying!* I want to scream at her. Can't you see that I'm the fuck-up here? That your job is to laugh at me, talk about me, pity me? Christ! I even let you fuck me today. Doesn't that count for anything? Doesn't that clarify who's on top of whom? But this all passes in less time than it takes to consider, for it is absurd, and I immediately assemble the support that I think she will require.

"Tell me what happened," I say, for evidently something of import did, indeed, happen.

"I really can't." Nervously looking around for but not finding a prop, she continues, "Um, I'll tell you what: I guess I just came out here to let you know that I'll be going away for a while." She's making up—no, deciding—this as she goes. "I'll get some things together and spend a few nights at Tony's house. Or maybe Pam is better. William, will you tell . . . whoever . . . that I'll be back in a few days and not to fuck with my room?"

"Sure," I say, at this point happy to be drifting with the current. Perhaps Pam will have whatever it is that Maggie couldn't find in the shed. "Were you in the shed a minute ago?"

"What shed?" she says sharply, betraying a slight annoyance that I should interrupt her life planning with a tedious physical inquiry.

Deciding to look for another way in: "Nothing, forget it."

But she abruptly and decidedly rises, and I watch her in deferential silence. The piecing of this puzzle, it is becoming apparent to me, will be done only after consulting Double Felix, for Maggie's reluctance to utter his name a moment ago serves as the X of a treasure map. I can wait; she is anxious to pursue her resolution of retreat.

"William, can I have some cab fare?" (a refreshingly wry grin here)

"Be my guest," I say, deliberately not adding where my money is kept.

Maggie trots off to my room and the top dresser drawer. We both know the money is there and we both know that Maggie knows the money is there. I'm pleased that she didn't go through the motion of asking me where it is. I'm pleased that our relationship maintains this level of integrity; it permits me to worry about her.

I suppose that Laurie's departure, delivered to me cloaked in Maggie's enigmatic tempest, is less of a disappointment to me than I might earlier have guessed. Though I have little doubt that it comes on the heels of what must have been a heavy scene, as well as presages one that, as such things tend to go, will be somewhat heavier, I feel strangely unaffected and complacent. I'm happy to sit out here and let these things come to pass. I'm happy too that Laurie is gone; she did seem something of an evil messenger, driving a wedge between Double Felix and me.

I wonder what I saw in her. Why was she attractive to me? In retrospect, and under the influence of coefficients gin, cold, and solitude, my infatuation with her surpassed what is normally indicated in the face of merely a piece of ass; that is to say the mere face of a pretty girl. I didn't attend that party for the spread; maybe I went just because I was invited. Maybe I shouldn't have gone at all.

There was (is?) in that girl a magnet of sorts, one naggingly germane to these environs but insistently closer to the source than I, for all my purported permanence, could ever be. This may have been the basis of my attraction, this apparent ticket to deeper places, places that would strengthen my already-too-secure purchase on this ever-shaky ground. The walls of this deck look closer now than any real walls could, and this is what I do. So, given this, given that I've folded my own map as a way to keep from getting lost, it's no wonder that I jumped on a chance to do it better, to do even this tiny place better, make it closer and own it well. Like a ballpoint on a newsprint maze, I went ahead and drew myself deeper into a channel that I knew to be a dead end, because it was preferable to the indignity of retreat, defeated by the inside back cover of *TV Week* or *Forty Puzzles 4-U!*, shameful blue retracings and crisscrosses left for everyone to see.

Tension, looming and about to slap my face, is what wheel squeaks loudest now that Laurie is gone. I need to wake up to Zipper; it is not only something that she wishes but something that I can do. I need to wake up and smell the coffee on the wall. I need to stand, I know I am ready, willing, and ready.

As such I am found, fleeting-so-no-harm-done snooze stopped short by a hand on my shoulder. I know it as Zipper's; the touch is unique and only for me, of this I am now certain. A formidable replacement and just in time, she is, for the now half, now all-but-all submerged sun. The sky cools pink and orange, and these colors are warm.

"You're here," she says, as if she was about to check off a minor item on a long list but can't seem to find the appropriate box.

"You say that as if I might be not-here," I more or less say. My rejoinder is alarmingly sloppy, and I burp adjunctly; the tariff on solitary drinking and the burp of a little girl. I take a deep drink, and Zipper sits rather than frowns. After waiting in vain for some elucidation, I add, "You expected me to be elsewhere?"

"I was not really thinking about it," she says, almost befuddled—if such a word could ever describe what Zipper almost is—yet still many steps ahead of me. "But Double Felix came into my room and said that I should come out here and talk to you. He said that you needed to talk to me and if you were not here that I should tell him right away." Zipper is wonderful in her capacity to accommodate the drunken whim. No doubt she draws on her experience with men primed to believe anything, the this-is-my-first-real-trick trick. "So we should talk. Do you want to talk?" she asks.

"Yeah, sure . . . but not urgently." This sounds bad, try: "What I mean is I don't know why Double Felix would tell you that. I haven't seen him for a while." Even as I say this I'm trying desperately to recall just when I did last speak to him and what exactly we spoke about; I thought I knew. When in doubt, be in doubt. I find myself increasingly unconcerned about the whens and whatevers of Double Felix.

Looking out to sea, she says carefully, "The house feels . . . old," and with this her eyes fall on me, without visible motion of the pupils, the way women recently of age learn to do: eyeball motion concealed with seductive eyelid dip. Zipper normally doesn't employ such gestures—or is her technique so fluent that I usually fail to detect them, falling instead guilelessly under their cumulative influence?

"Oh?" I say, wondering if she knows that Laurie and Maggie are gone, or even Timmy. For some reason this last requires an immediate answer. "Did you know that Timmy left?" I am diffident—and for some reason exclusive—here, for we may have already discussed his departure. "And Laurie . . . and Maggie," I add, and the afterthought format I ended up with makes me, I fear, sound pathetic, weak, and deceitful. Actually, if I didn't know better I'd think I was a schoolboy on a first date, hopelessly caught in the current, overly anxious, blowing it, swirling, nearing the drain. I tack on a mealymouthed, "That is, for a while, maybe. Maggie's gone for a few days, but she might come back."

Behind her eyes now, though there is no external evidence of it, there is some fearsome evaluation—reevaluation?—taking place, not that I would ever, or could ever, be privy to such things. "I did feel a distillation," she says distractedly, a foreground task to divert my attention from this surreptitious background processing.

Oh, please! I want to sardonically moan, suddenly—or perhaps just now realizing that I am—jealous of her femininity. Instead I say, "A distillation? What's that mean? I fucking felt a distillation. What kind of Third World laboratory voodoo line is that?" I start to laugh, feeling that I can bring her along with me, for she is smiling despite herself.

But I am cut short by a visceral feeling of trepidation. We both sense it and look to each other for confirmation.

"Something's fucked up," I say.

"There's a fire," she says.

Far too quickly the flames, licking the periphery of our surprise and sucking our hearts toward the hot vacuum of panic, appear dancing about the floor of the hall with an unnatural ease that betrays the hand of a man. I wrestle with a brief period of denial, refusing to believe that our first avenue of escape is no longer. It seems that I should have at least had the opportunity to hesitate, frozen in fear, and render myself solely responsible for our evident entrapment. But no, this way would have been closed to the fleetest of foot, and so I am denied a blame that I would have, perversely, preferred. Of course there is the hill behind us, treacherous though still negotiable, especially in circumstances such as these. It may be this knowledge that tempers my alarm; more likely it is a stubborn refusal to believe in The Dire Emergency, specifically those such as this, which come upon one without warning and are the stuff of which local coming-up-at-eleven news trailers are made. Such action-cam reports are purely popular fiction to me, light fare. I choose to reserve my consternation for the hellfire of my private brooding and the long, slow screw of the beating heart.

Double Felix!

"We can't get to him through here," I say, dispensing with the antecedental prompt. Zipper is always a step ahead of me, and this is a good time to factor that into our conversation.

Expectably, she just looks at me expectantly. I've grown used to these little tests, for they are part of her nature, and this one in particular is marked, not only because of the context, but also because of her very visible desire to have me and me alone deal with the situation. Indeed, I believe she would stand here and die if such was the product of my engineering. I pull at my gin bottle, somehow, mercifully in my hand, though I don't recall picking it up. She takes this in impatiently but without any real disdain

Pointedly she says, "What should we do?"

For the moment the flames are content with the painted drywall and varnished parquet of the hallway. There is no encroachment out onto the deck; perhaps the wood has imbibed too much of the airborne Pacific, but I doubt it. I think this pasture is just not yet green enough in the company of the oh-so-very flammable interior. This will pass as that dwindles. Soon Zipper and I will be slipping over the railing of the deck, and thus leaving the house, a thought which fills me with dread; so much so that the rescue of Double Felix is a more palatable alternative—morally and selfishly.

"You'll have to go over the railing," I say. Actually, I shout it, though I don't know why as the fire isn't causing any great roar just yet; I guess television has disinclined me from a normal speaking voice under such circumstances. "You're probably agile as a fucking Peruvian mountain goat anyway." Leading her by the arm to the edge of the deck, I point down and around to the south. "You should go down about ten feet then climb back up on that side of the house . . ." I'm interrupted by the sound of approaching sirens, and looking down, we both see a pair of fire trucks turning off of PCH onto the canyon road. "Fuck!" I say.

"What?" she says, and I realize that not only did my voice drop, but as if not to disappoint me, the fire is murmuring aggressively, well on its way to a textbook roar.

"It must be pretty bad in front for them to be on their way already," I say, though only now is an inordinate amount of smoke filling the sky. "Someone must have called this in a few minutes ago. Maybe Double Felix! Maybe he's in front." Now helping her over the railing: "In any case, you'll probably be greeted at the side of the house when you get back up."

But she is reluctant and, I think, a wee bit frightened. "I don't understand. If he's already out front, then where are you going? You can't go in there," she says, pointing to the hall and shaking her head.

Her hair flies dramatically back and forth, befitting the drama, and the thought of that hair in flames strikes a gelid note of real terror to my own heart. I feel mobilized, and helplessly theatrical, woefully caught up in the making of a memory. I can't fucking believe I could be so very attentive under such distracting circumstances.

"I'm going over the balconies to his room. There is absolutely no reason for you to come with me!"

This of course is not true: I'd go with her. But we both realize that I'm the one who needs a face-slapping, and it is to her credit that, in making the more difficult-to-bear choice, she assents. She kisses my arm and starts down the hill. Alone, I taste of hard and hot fear. I turn to the hall, and the fire moves out to greet me.

To my left is the first of seven tile walls configured as partitions that separate the private balconies for each of the six guest rooms. Unlike the ground under this deck, which Zipper is now negotiating, the hill falls off quite sharply under the balconies. To make matters worse, they were constructed to be quite seclusive and hence extend outward with a fair overhang. My plan is to move from balcony to balcony, railing to railing, by swinging around each of these tile walls in turn.

I managed this once around a single wall some many months back. Very drunk and mischievous at one of the more protracted parties, I had been soliciting the attentions of an attractive albeit surly looking woman. Getting nowhere but drunker, I at last came up and presented the idea that she make love to me rather brutally, to the point of strangling me dead at the moment of orgasm. I doubt that I was really serious, but I probably would have gone through with it had she been game; how far, I truly don't know. Be that as it may, she of course refused to take me seriously, so rather than bore her further, I solemnly vowed to her that I would go directly to my room, masturbate in her name, and, at the moment of ejaculation, leap from my balcony. This I did, ceremoniously and loudly locking the door behind, then actually standing upright on my railing and jerking off, and though I came all over the steep embankment, no one came to my door. Somehow, in the throes of sanctimony and intoxication, I had myself looking forward to a door-breaking climax complete with a carnal denouement. It didn't happen. Wounded, I remembered that the room next to mine was currently vacant, and since I had boyishly often considered the possibility, I took advantage of my halfway-there condition on the railing, and accomplished the crossing. I landed moments later on the hard floor of the neighboring balcony, sweaty, terrified, and bruised from the last-second desperate bail houseward. Here I waited—I have no idea how long—until I realized that nobody was even missing me, much less looking for me. In mid crossing I had relinquished my glass to the moisture-starved dust of the hill, and eventually the dearth of drink got to me. From the bar in that room I could hear that it was business as usual outside the door, so I simply rejoined the party, which was now sans surly bitch who had wisely split, and never related the adventure to anyone.

Now faced with a much more attentive executioner, I rather long for a replay of the mere drunken stroll which that whole episode turned out to be. The fire, I notice, isn't advancing any more slowly, so I move directly to the first wall. Next to the deck, it is the balcony of my own neglected room that lies on the other side; now I shall visit it. The heat emanating from the fire lends an alien quality to the moist, dew-covered surface of the tile, adding to my growing feeling of separateness from the house. More than merely physically, I am truly outside of this house now. It's a new and unusually thrilling sensation for me, one I had all but forgotten during my time here. Clammy hands on either side of the dewy tile wall, I grip as tightly as the slickness will allow and hoist myself up to a standing position on the railing. With a start I discover a smile on my lips; I too am at my do point. I brace myself, ready to swing the bulk of my weight like a pendulum, my arms the chain, the wall the logical center around which all my motion must be considered, the whole business colored perfectly within the inexorable lines of

Newtonian intervention, the philosophy of physics: I think therefore I swing. With a resolve that can't help but seem tentatively tempered, I push away from the deck. I glimpse the fire, tag a pang in gut—separation anxiety.

Out, Away, Over. At the apogee of this maneuver—that is, the point at which my ass is farthest from the house—there is a moment of disengagement between my feet and the respective railings. I don't recall this from my previous experience out here—that amounted to more of a leap, blinded by the spurious confidence of a one-time shot—but my right foot is required to push away from the deck railing an instant before my left foot contacts the balcony railing. At this moment I become acutely aware of the dewy liquid buffer between my hands and the tile, for it is the most solid matter holding me to the house, and while it does feel arisen to the occasion with the added viscosity of terror, it isn't what keeps me where I need to be; that function is performed—I know—by the sheer gravity of the house. Here I meet face to fact either a streak of insanity or the force to which I have succumbed for lo these many months. The difference is negligible. Whether insanity or perception, outside force or inside enforceability, I finally see it because I finally pulled away from it. I am over the first wall, and I jump down onto the balcony for a brief rest. My room is dark except for a dim orange glow under the inside door. Resisting a very strong urge to slip inside for a quick drink and what would become the longest of naps, I mount the railing again and prepare for the second wall.

Over. This time the hop over to the next balcony is too easy; in fact, I really don't attend to it, as if it were done in a drunken blackout. This balcony, this room, is Zipper's. I connect it with her, for it is the room she's had since her arrival, and this house is the only place I've known her. I can't look through the doors for fear of seeing her possessions and her domain engulfed in flames, though I know she wouldn't entertain such foolishness. I can't imagine her ever growing attached to things, a weakness I once had and will certainly have again. Zipper knows them to be impossibly ethereal. I too have felt this in some of my more cherished objects, such as my Rolex—dear to me in part, ironically, because of its mechanical permanence and independence—which seduced me only when I discovered a model cloaked not in gold or platinum but in stainless steel, a platonic encasement befitting the internal preciosity that bespeaks the gearing of time. I try to look away from her room, but a flash of a bright red pillow cries out to me, an inanimate SOS launched to the corner of my unsuspecting eye. Again I feel moved to enter the house, this time to rescue the pillow, to risk my life for the honor of retrieving something that she may be remotely fond of. Now I see the glow of flames, and I dare not go in peeping pursuit of the source. It looked a bit more intense than what I saw playing outside my own door; whether hers was closed or not, I don't know. A tear needlessly rises to my eye. Zipper's balcony is turning out to be a perilous place emotionally as well as obviously. I remain on the railing, cross to the third wall.

Out, Away . . . Over. Not quite as easy as the second, my hands, first right then left, slip at the crucial moment in response to the inertia. By the ease of my second I was lulled into thinking that these crossings might be easier than I had anticipated; but no harm is done. I hop down, nevertheless, to the balcony that lies outside of Maggie's room. I can see into it quite clearly, for her door was definitely left open, and the fire is well established inside the room. But it doesn't look like there's much to burn in there. Evidently Maggie embarked on more of a long-term absence than she indicated, for her belongings are not in sight, and Maggie's belongings were always kept very much in sight. The sudden pop of a discarded aerosol can snaps my attention to the area under her dresser. It is littered with various Maggie-type effects—lipsticks, Kleenexes, and all type of feminine product guaranteed to cause titters in any men's locker room—and it is very clear to me now that she left in a hurry and without much method to her sadness. I could have done better by her. I think I would now. Before turning back to the railing, I notice that the sliding glass door to her balcony is set open about an inch. Surely a moot point at this late hour, but this seems to be a needless supply of oxygen for the fire, and I foolishly move to close it. So proud am I to have thought of this that I disregard the warning aura of heat from the glass and grasp full and fast the handle of the aluminum door. Perhaps as a manifestation of shock, my mind is instantly filled with speculation about the probable melting point of aluminum, and how the fuck could something this hot remain solid. I have sustained my first injury from the fire; wincing and hopping around, swearing and growling, I am nonetheless happy—or sure that I will be—to have met the foe and survived. Such is the whim our minds are given to during moments of savagery. With our bodies mobilized by pain or fear into a darker and more efficient mode, our minds have nothing special to do, nowhere to go. Suddenly they are the feckless assistants to the tolerant master. I feel too far from this, think Timmy could do better and wish he were here, take the railing and face the fourth wall.

Out, Away . . . My best grip on these things has been only good enough; that was without a burned right. But then this is a pretty minor injury, I a pretty major baby. The trick here is to press and clench tightly of the wall as if there were no pain. This I do, and it adds to the perverse exhilaration that plays in my stomach less like a butterfly and more like an unmanned fire hose, nips my ass every time I swing out and around. The fourth wall frightens me. I could be a big, white-lettered sign, reading ENDOFTHELINE instead of HOLLYWOODLAND. I have a pre-monition of myself plunged downward, back broken and bleeding to death in a prickly thicket, the erstwhile object of a nonplussed search party, laughing above while breaking for doughnuts and flirting with Zipper. . . . *Over*, cackling from a handheld radio.

My burned hand sticks like hot glue, a strikingly uncomfortable simile, and I land with a lunge on the balcony of Timmy's vacant room. I feel unwelcome here, as if the house has passed the point of hoping for a cessation to its own demise and now wishes to be left alone during such a very private affair; or maybe it's just that I'm on Timmy's balcony. I am an alien organism, a fetus too long in the womb. Timmy's ex-room is the most conflagrant yet, but the fire is confining itself to only the walls. It is an eerie sight, a cinematic room of flames that looks life-sustaining at its center. Of course there wouldn't be much oxygen to be had there, and this could be limiting the migration of the flames to the bed and furniture. I wish I knew more of such things; I wish I were able to second-guess the fire. I can only assume that things are worsening in all areas of the house. Double Felix's room may even now be overpriced kindling, but then Double Felix himself may be safely outside, although I don't feel this. I don't feel this at all. Mounting the railing, I take the fifth wall.

OutAwayOver. Becoming familiar, inasmuch as such things can ever be familiar, this crossing passes without incident—but again that sounds trite, for such things are intrinsically singular, repetition not-withstanding; I'm not that adaptable. To make up some time, I choose not to rest on the balcony, gaining instead the same ground with a few perilous strides along the railing. This room has been empty for quite some time, and as I glance into it I see that it is utterly dark. I so expected to see the fiercest burning yet that the absence of anything wrong almost bowls me off the railing, as if I had turned and encountered a gorilla or a snowstorm. I pause, trying to discern even the faintest glow from under the inside door, but the room is as yet totally unaffected. I am at once disturbed by the incongruity and hopeful of Double Felix's safety. I can almost feel him in his room now. Two more walls to cross, one more room, Laurie's, I have at it.

Out. Away? Back. The wall inflames my already sensitive hand. Though a tentative touch with the other confirms that it is merely warm, this development is at best worrisome, and I doubt that Laurie's room—dare I say her hotbed?—will be the mundane affair of the previous. Nothing now if not committed, I press on. There should be nothing on her balcony that could fuel a fire; nonetheless I peek around the wall before swinging fully around it. All clear, and I realize how foolish I've been to not manage this tiny precaution at the other walls. Over. I go over badly, slipping and barking my right knee on the railing and subsequently knocking my jaw against the wall. A mass of limbs and disbelief, I not so dramatically regain my purchase without much trouble and not so heroically flop over the railing onto Laurie's balcony. Instinctively reaching for my face, I feel wetness, and a bit of dirty blood rides my hand back away for my secretly pleased inspection: my best battle scar yet. Zipper will be overcome with smarmy effusion and silent pledges to never let me out of her sight again. Before me I see why the wall was heated. The room is entirely engulfed in flames, and the heat emanating from the plate-glass doors pushes me back against the railing. Loud too, the fire here burns with the advantage of a door set open six inches on the balcony and another fully swung at the hallway. I'm somewhat mesmerized by the enormity, the in-your-face quality of these flames. They have efficiently given no quarter. Laurie's long gone, with no knowledge of these heated events, but here or not, as things stand now, there is absolutely no trace of that girl left in this room. The contrast with the adjoining room is almost preternatural, as if the very space that Laurie occupied is perfect fuel for the fire. So be it. I really don't want to hang around here; hot glass doors undoubtedly pose some sort of threat—information now lost to me, buried irretrievably in an ash heap of public service announcements. Double Felix awaits, one last wall away.

Out . . . This one's easy, for on the other side is not a balcony but a gentle slope of dirt that precedes the precipitous drop overlooked by the balconies. Left geometrically to fend for itself by the irregular shape and offset location of Double Felix's balcony, it's the only relatively flat land on this side of the house. I know well this few feet of open space, having spent many an hour staring at it from that balcony during Morning Vodka . . . and Down. I go to it, swinging around and down with a thud on the uninvolved dirt. First glance, rising slowly and theatrically from a crouch to a full stand, the room is quiet and—surprisingly—dark. I'm feeling stunningly athletic and agile, befitting my cause. My body is willing to go along with this, and it is with an easy Burroughsian leap that I gain this final objective, Double Felix's private balcony.

Only now do I realize that Double Felix's room is dark because the entire house is dark. At some point during my iterative hop-around-the-house the power must have gone out. This means nothing but is still enough of an unexpected development to make me realize that I have no real plan. I stand in the dark, momentarily unsure of how to proceed and preparing to start nonetheless by bellowing out his name while chucking a chair at a window. I don't even know if the sliding doors are latched; I'm reluctant to try my hand at one. I feel disoriented and befuddled, out of my league. I guess I thought that all I had to do was get here, that Double Felix would be clinging desperately to the edge of his conflagrant balcony, crying out for succor, for me. But I should have known that in the real world as well as the fictive, such scenes demand the participation of a woman.

A muffled grunt. A sliding glass door shatters itself. Then another, this time with the help of an axe which retracts almost before I see it. It all happens very fast, many things crowding a single moment, and I stand at the ready at the far side of the balcony.

"Whoa! Hell, I didn't expect to find anyone out here!" This from a firefighter, tall and big in hat and coat, and as startled to discover me as I am at being discovered. He hollers excitedly over his shoulder, "Hey, I got one!" Then to me: "I didn't hit you with any broken glass, did I? Come with me; we've got a way out the front for you."

I numbly follow, a bit too stunned to talk. I suppose I know that if these guys are here then Double Felix must be safe and sound, or at least the matter is out of my hands. Still, I look furtively around his room as we pass through it like a parent inspecting the proudly displayed work of his child, not wanting to hurt anybody's feelings. Only one other fireman is haunting the area, though I now hear shouting and voices from the front. Double Felix's room is pretty thoroughly trashed, black everywhere, raining oil-slicked water, some punky spots generating little clouds of steam and smoke. More than anything it looks timed, like everything burned evenly but only for a short while. Many things, having lost their color, still have their shape. Of course it's all a new experience for me; I've never strolled through a fire before, and the effect of this pervasive damage is profound. It seems almost willful, as if directed by an intelligence. I'm amazed that so much transpired here during the short(?) time that I was coming around the house.

"Is there a girl out front?" I ask. "A man?"

He either pats or pushes me on the shoulder. "Yeah, don't worry, she's out there. I think she'll be happy to see you too. She seemed to think that you were inside the house."

I am led through the big room, conventionally via the hall. The front door is closed, but cut through the middle of it is a square hole. To this I am directed, a gloved hand waiting on the other side.

"This opens, you know," I say, but it only gets me tugged through a bit more harshly.

Looking dour and accusative, the man on the other side grabs my hands and pulls them up to his nose, then reading my face, he lets them down gently. He is somewhat rustic looking and wears his badge loudly.

"Who are you?" he says in a way that echoes: you'd better get this right!

I hear a squeal, and turning, I see Zipper running to me from across the driveway. "I'm with her," I simply say, pointing.

"Oh, yeah," he says, surprisingly. "Well, step back . . . Wait." Putting a finger on my chin, he bellows into my face, "MED! We'll take a look at that cut. You'll both step back now, please."

Zipper hits me like a wave and clutches painfully, silently. "Do you know how it started?" I ask him as he turns away.

Turning back, annoyed, he scrunches up his nose as one does when smelling demonstratively. "Don't you have a nose, boy?" he asks.

"Yes," I say lamely, even looking first at Zipper, still buried in my side, as if for confirmation.

More visible sniffing. "Gasoline!" he says, his voice crisp as the night air.

EPILOGUE

T he deck is black but seemingly solid. The house is none too colorful, and due to the possibility of a compromise in the structural
integrity we've been advised to stay outside by the fire chief, or at
least the chief-on-scene, a woman who emerged at fire's end from under the damaged roof and an oxygen mask, quietly dispensing orders
and doing whatever gets done. It is very late. The sun may be rising
soon—I don't know; my Rolex slipped away at some point during my
daring and ineffectual rescue. Double Felix was not found, neither alive
nor dead. I suggested that a search of the hillside be made, and two
men were dispatched for a short while, but this effort, though deemed
adequate by the police, was really just a halfhearted reflection of their
belief that Double Felix was the arsonist and as such has absconded.
Zipper is down the hill on an errand. I wasn't ready yet to leave here,
so she went reluctantly without me. She should be back soon, and I'm
okay with sitting out here and waiting for her, alone.

As I had earlier removed then subsequently lost the last bottle of gin
from the bar out here, I am now forced to drink vodka, Double Felix's
drink of choice for me, and in this I find a melancholy artistry that is
well suited for me, a would-be artist who would willingly be melancholy.
In my hand is a photo strip, the sort dispensed by automated booths just
inside the doors of dilapidated Woolworth's stores. Produced by Zipper

after a surreptitious post-policeandfire search of what was Double Felix's room (we were admonished to not touch anything), it portrays in triplicate Double Felix and a very young girl whom we instantly recognized as a very young Laurie. The striking resemblance between the two then-innocent faces, though now somewhat mitigated by age, is still so obvious that I was amazed we hadn't noticed earlier, but then Double Felix and Laurie were never together all that much, not at all really. Stunned, I stared at the pictures while Zipper ducked away sheepishly to look for car keys, no doubt embarrassed at being caught out of the loop, as it were. On an impulse that was felt more by her than by myself, she went down the hill to a nearby always-open, always-sleazy motel to look for Laurie and give her news of the fire. After all, Laurie may be heir to this bit of charred and humbled turf.

The other day a man in the San Fernando Valley murdered his wife and children, then himself. This story came on the heels of a similar tragedy across the country in Louisiana about a week earlier. Tonight I was asked—more chatty than business—by a momentarily idle policeman if Double Felix had perhaps been trying to murder his family. I told him that I doubted it as I knew of no family. The cop seemed relieved and walked away, and I was left wondering about the ticks and tocks of the family clocks on the walls of those houses in the Valley and in the South. What is it that happens inside of a man during those final moments in the mirror? Does he think of how he'll be treated by the media? After blowing away every shred of love in sight, does he then turn the gun on himself as part of an act of contrition? Or is it, regardless of the plan, really the most effective way to eliminate his pain? I think the murders are ultimately a way to lend credibility to the suicide. I think they are a way to force a hand.

Double Felix, now more ardently enigmatic than ever, simply

stopped chewing. I don't think anyone died here tonight. During these years, before and after my participation, I think something of old was emulated, and a work of art was drawn; then abandoned. Things worked well, as they are apt to do, but then Laurie came here. The new legitimacy wasn't so damn tenable anymore. Matter touched antimatter, and it all summed to zero.

These events are now banished to my past. As such they have achieved some distance, never to be truly measured, always far because I can never again go there, always near because that is the nature of our memories. My world and everything I kept in my one worldly basket is now distilled down to a key with no door and a waning few inches of vodka.

Yes, there is a front door key in my pocket—not that the door was ever locked or I ever likely to be on the far side of it. I insisted on it the day I realized just how valuable this place would become to me, that I could never face being locked out, that I was never going to leave. Double Felix could find no existing key, not even one of his own, and he had to have a new lock installed just so that I could have a key to it. It's here in my pocket; it's my only key. I don't think I saw the paradox at the time, but I insisted just the same.

Zipper doesn't know about this key, but then it is a trivial matter, not the sort of thing that one would classify as a secret. She is everything that I feel I cannot be, and in that sense she may be more than I can do. I don't know, for we have never been together outside the confines of this house. I realize now that, for a while at least, I will be very dependent on her, and that's okay with me; it feels natural.

"I am back," she says from behind me, appearing on the deck silently, as if on cat paws or under sublime wings, as if in response to my invocation.

A thin wisp of smoke rises from a crack across the deck but immediately vanishes into the ocean breeze. I ache in many places, but
the pain has turned the corner and yielded to the satisfying soreness
of healing.

"Any luck? Any Laurie?" I ask, hoping not, hoping that she and I
can commence our solitude.

She sits next to me on one of two chairs that I salvaged from the
kitchen. My chaise is MIA, perhaps swept over the hill in a torrent of
high-pressure city water on its way to meet the extremely high-pressure
salty water.

"She was there, but the man did not know if it was tonight or last
night. This I expected." She looks at me with a raised eyebrow, like I
was the one withholding facts. "I did not expect to get even this little
bit when I asked him, but he wanted to know about the fire trucks. This
motel—maybe she went there with Timmy last night—this motel is not
a place of great loyalty."

I have the ridiculous urge to vow that I will never visit the place.
Part of my enthusiasm, such as it is, for whatever turn my life is taking
is the need to assert it all over the place in as many ways as possible.
Overkill. I want to make my commitment then fry it black. I want to be
ten years old. I used to stand around the kitchen as my mother cooked,
so in love with her and just discovering the frustration that goes with
love. I would cling to her: not enough. Stand away and speak: "Mom?"
I would say. "What," she faithfully responded. "Nothing," my lame response as I tried rubbing my eyes to see what adventures in attention it
might bring. "Mom?" "What." "Nothing." "Mom?" "What." "Nothing."
Mom-What-Nothing. MomWhatNothing. Zipper needs this about as
much as my mother did. Of course, I was a sharp kid and got the picture
way back then; it didn't stop me.

"I'll never go there," I say, at once exasperated and full of pride at having come up with this thing to say.

"Where?" she says, still not finished with the Laurie story and not really listening.

"Nothing. So what should we do about Laurie?" I ask.

Obviously having worked this over already in her own head, she says, "We have done it already. Even as I was asking about her I knew that I was going too far. She will know about the fire. She can get whatever information she needs. Remember that she left here for her own reasons. She does not need us running after her."

"Yes, well it's up to you. This is a call that you're infinitely better equipped to make." Sipping my vodka, I rock the chair back on two legs and secretly pine for my chaise. I feel speciously satisfied with this resolution, like I've just shut off the flashlight and come out from under the covers after a long night of scrutinizing a pilfered *Playboy* magazine. Zipper is right, and I am through wondering after Laurie.

Zipper shivers and squeezes my arm. We are next to each other. We are parts of a whole. I could make love to her now, but I think we'll wait for a higher ground; this deck and this house are spent. There will never be any real provocative passion here again, at least not for us, the formerly formally established occupants, and I see now that there hasn't been for quite some time. The sex acts here have been hollow, charged only with guesses and performances, cheap attempts at communications that should have been verbal, not oral. Soon Zipper and I will leave here with the night, get some digs and be together. Unlike myself, she has maintained something of a real life outside of the house—friends, checkbooks, and such—and I am given to understand that we will not be entirely destitute. For me, of course, a modicum of destitution may be in order, but not to worry: that sort of thing goes with the territory.

The water is indeed very big. Leaning forward, I kiss her cinnamon cheek. She lets me—a small victory known only to me. I am seated back, looking at the spot upon which my lips landed. Only a just-then ago our bodies touched (witness the salty spoil still on my lips), and I knew the exquisite texture of her skin. What luck! What a perfect little event! I could do it again. She's still there, hasn't moved yet. I could lean forward in the same subtle way, steal another kiss and maybe even touch her briefly with the tip of my tongue as my lips distract. I could do it again easy. I could do it . . . until she tells me to stop.

Also available from Akashic Books

LAS VEGAS NOIR
edited by Jarret Keene & Todd James Pierce
320 pages, trade paperback original, $15.95

Brand-new stories by: John O'Brien, David Corbett, Scott Phillips, Nora Pierce, Tod Goldberg, Felicia Campbell, Pablo Medina, Christine McKellar, Lori Kozlowski, Vu Tran, Celeste Starr, Preston L. Allen, and others.

"Just because mystery fans will be unfamiliar with many of the sixteen contributors to Akashic's latest entry in its acclaimed Noir Series doesn't mean the quality isn't up to volumes boasting bigger names. The late John O'Brien, best known for his novel-turned-film, *Leaving Las Vegas,* offers a typically warped and nihilistic vision of the city with 'The Tik,' about a thrill-killing duo, narrated by the male half, whose indifference to his prey is chilling . . . This anthology does a fine job of illuminating the dark underbelly of Sin City." —*Publishers Weekly*

LOS ANGELES NOIR
edited by Denise Hamilton
360 pages, trade paperback original, $15.95
*A *Los Angeles Times* best seller and winner of an Edgar Award.

Brand-new stories by: Michael Connelly, Janet Fitch, Susan Straight, Patt Morrison, Robert Ferrigno, Gary Phillips, Naomi Hirahara, Jim Pascoe, and others.

"Akashic is making an argument about the universality of noir; it's sort of flattering, really, and *Los Angeles Noir,* arriving at last, is a kaleidoscopic collection filled with the ethos of noir pioneers Raymond Chandler and James M. Cain."
—*Los Angeles Times Book Review*

DEMONS IN THE SPRING
short stories by Joe Meno w/original illustrations by twenty artists
282 pages, limited edition hardcover, $24.95
*A finalist for the Story Prize

Original artwork by: Charles Burns, Laura Owens, Cody Hudson, Ivan Brunetti, Jay Ryan, Jon Resh, Paul Hornschemeier, Anders Nilsen, and others.

"The strongest stories in this collection don't try too hard to dazzle with formal virtuosity but let Meno slowly pull his characters out from their own peculiar inner worlds into the one we recognize, for better or for worse, as the real world. Loss seems to be the lingua franca that unites these souls; Meno's sympathy for them is acute, and he never lets fictional pyrotechnics blind him, or us, to their humanity."
—*New York Times*

THE AGE OF DREAMING
a novel by Nina Revoyr
328 pages, trade paperback original, $15.95
*A finalist for the *Los Angeles Times* Book Prize

"Rare indeed is a novel this deeply pleasurable and significant."
—*Booklist* (starred review)

"Reminiscent of Paul Auster's *The Book of Illusions* in its concoction of spurious Hollywood history and its star's filmography, but Revoyr is a more ingenuous writer than Auster . . ." —*San Francisco Chronicle*

SOUTHLAND
a novel by Nina Revoyr
348 pages, trade paperback original, $15.95
*Winner of the Lambda, Ferro-Grumley, and ALA Stonewall awards; a *Los Angeles Times* best seller; Edgar finalist; *Los Angeles Times* "Best Books of 2003" list.

"The plot line of *Southland* is the stuff of a James Ellroy or a Walter Mosley novel . . . But the climax fairly glows with the good-heartedness that Revoyr displays from the very first page." —*Los Angeles Times Book Review*

"Fascinating and heartbreaking . . . an essential part of L.A. history."
—*L.A. Weekly*

HIGH LIFE
a novel by Matthew Stokoe, with an introduction by Dennis Cooper
336 pages, trade paperback original, $15.95
*A selection of Dennis Cooper's Little House on the Bowery series

"Stokoe's in-your-face prose and raw, unnerving scenes give way to a skillfully plotted tale that will keep readers glued to the page." —*Publishers Weekly*

"Summer Sizzlers: Page-turning books that will keep you glued to your beach blankets . . . Soaked in such graphic detail that the pages smell, Stokoe's *High Life* is the sickest revision of the California crime novel, ever." —*Paper Magazine*

IFICW   OBRIE

O'BRIEN, JOHN
BETTER